The Seagull

The Seagull

A play by Anton Chekhov

Translated by David French

(Notes by Donna Orwin)

Talonbooks   •   Vancouver   •   1993

Translation copyright © 1977, 1978, 1993 David French
Notes © 1978 Donna Orwin

Talonbooks
P.O. Box 2076, Vancouver, British Columbia, Canada V6B 3S3
www.talonbooks.com

Typeset in New Baskerville and printed and bound in Canada.
Printed on 100% post-consumer recycled paper.

Fifth printing: August 2012

The publisher gratefully acknowledges the financial support of the
Canada Council for the Arts, the Government of Canada through the
Canada Book Fund and the Province of British Columbia through the
British Columbia Arts Council and the Book Publishing Tax Credit for
our publishing activities.

First published in 1978 by General Publishing Co. Ltd., Don Mills, Ontario.

Canadian Cataloguing in Publication Data

Chekhov, Anton Pavlovich, 1860–1904.
    The seagull

    Translation of: Chaika
    ISBN 0-88922-324-6

    I. French, David 1939–   II. Title.
PG3456.C5F713 1993   891.72'3   C93-091210-1

The Seagull was produced by the National Actors Theatre and performed at the Lyceum Theatre on Broadway in New York, New York, November 17, 1992 - January 10, 1993 with the following cast:

ARKADINA	Tyne Daly
CONSTANTINE	Ethan Hawke
SORIN	John Franklyn-Robbins
NINA	Laura Linney
SHAMRAYEV	Russel Lunday
POLINA	Joan MacIntosh
MASHA	Maryann Plunkett
TRIGORIN	Jon Voight
DORN	Tony Roberts
MEDVEDENKO	Zane Lasky
YAKOV	Danny Burstein
COOK	John Beal
SERVANTS	Kam Metcalf
	Kevin Shinick, David Watson

Directed by Marshall W. Mason

Executive Producer Manny Kladitis
Settings by Marjorie Bradley Kellogg
Sound by Stewart Werner & Chuck London
Costumes by Laura Crow
Lighting by Richard Nelson

THE CHARACTERS

Irina Nikolayevna Arkadina, married name Treplyova,
an actress
Constantine Gavrilovich Treplyov (also Gavrilych), her
son, also known as Kostya
Peter Nikolayevich Sorin, her brother
Nina Zarechnaya, a young girl, daughter of a rich landowner
Ilya Shamrayev, a retired army lieutenant who manages
Sorin's estate
Polina, his wife
Masha, his daughter
Boris Alekseyevich Trigorin, a writer
Yevgeny Sergeyevich Dorn (also Sergeich), a doctor
Semyon Medvedenko, a schoolmaster
Yakov, a workman
Cook
Maid

THE PLACE

The action takes place in Sorin's house and garden.

THE TIME

There is an interval of two years between Act Three and Act
Four.

INTRODUCTION

It seems logical to me that Canadians should perform plays in Canadian translations and that these translations should be made by theatre craftsmen — actors, directors or, best of all, playwrights. As far as I know, very few serious translations have found their way into the repertory of the Canadian theatre. The usual practice has been to fall back upon an American or English translation or to assemble a composite text from the best of these. I did this when I directed *A Doll's House* in 1973 and I experienced enormous frustration because I couldn't test my arbitrary decisions against Ibsen's original Norwegian. The text was playable but something was missing — a distinctive flavour or perhaps a feeling of wholeness.

When I was planning to stage a production of Chekhov's *The Seagull*, I wanted a translation with this sense of wholeness. I thought immediately of David French, whose Mercer family plays suggest a strong affinity between his sensibility and that of Chekhov. Because *The Seagull* deals specifically with the whys and wherefores of being a writer and of working in the theatre, I sensed that he would be the right person to tackle the play.

Like many of the British and American writers who have translated *The Seagull*, David French is not a Russian scholar. He neither reads nor writes the language, but he steeped himself in Chekhov's stories and letters. In addition, he worked closely with Donna Orwin, a Tolstoy scholar, who challenged him on the tone and meaning of every word. During the early weeks of rehearsal he listened to the actors, and with Donna's assistance he altered the text to satisfy their combined passion for accuracy without compromising the play's theatrical vitality. I feel the translation is faithful to the spirit of the play, particularly in the way it emphasizes Chekhov's sense of comedy.

· Many who saw the production were excited by the clarity and freshness of the text, which managed to be uniquely Canadian without losing contact with Chekhov's Russia. David French's translation made this possible.

Bill Glassco
Tarragon Theatre
August 1977

ACT ONE

The grounds on SORIN's estate. A wide path leads into the park to a lake in the background. A makeshift stage has been erected across the path, blocking the view of the lake. There are bushes on either side of the stage. A few chairs and a small table.[1]

The sun has just set. Behind the lowered curtain on stage YAKOV and other workmen can be heard hammering and coughing. MASHA and MEDVEDENKO enter left, returning from a walk.

MEDVEDENKO:
Why do you always wear black?

MASHA:
I'm mourning my life. I'm unhappy.

MEDVEDENKO:
Why?   *(He thinks.)*   I don't understand . . .
You're healthy. Your father's not rich but he's comfortable. My life's a lot harder than yours. I only get twenty-three rubles a month, and that's before the pension is deducted. But I don't go around in mourning. *(They sit down.)*

MASHA:
It's not a question of money. A poor man can still be happy.

MEDVEDENKO:
In theory, perhaps, but not in practice. There's me, my mother, my two sisters and my little brother, and a salary of only twenty-three rubles. And you have to eat and drink. You need tea and sugar, don't you? And tobacco? It's a tight squeeze.[2]

MASHA: *(glancing towards the stage)*
The play'll start soon.

MEDVEDENKO:
Yes. Nina Zarechnaya will act in Constantine's play. They're in love, and their souls will merge tonight to create a single artistic image. But our souls have no point of contact. I love you. I'm so wretched I can't stay home. Every day I walk four miles here and four miles back, and all I get from you is indifferentism.[3] It's understandable. I have no means, we're a big family . . . Who'd want to marry a man who can't feed himself?

MASHA:
Rubbish. *(takes a pinch of snuff)* I'm touched by your love, but I can't return it, that's all. *(offers him the snuffbox)* Have some.

MEDVEDENKO:
I'd rather not. *(pause)*

MASHA:
It's stifling. There'll be a storm, most likely. All you do is philosophize or talk about money. You think the worst thing is being poor, but I think it's a thousand times easier to wear rags and beg than . . . But you'd never understand . . .

Enter SORIN and TREPLYOV, right.

SORIN: *(leaning on his walking stick)*
You see, my boy, the country . . . somehow it doesn't suit me, and . . . it's understandable . . . I could never

get used to it. Last night I went to bed at ten and woke up this morning at nine, feeling my brain was stuck to my skull from all that sleep . . . if you know what I mean. *(laughs)* But after lunch I dropped off again, unexpectedly, and now I'm a wreck . . . it's a nightmare, really . . .

TREPLYOV:
You're right, Uncle, you ought to live in town. *(sees MASHA and MEDVEDENKO)* Look, you're not supposed to be here. We'll call you when the play begins. So would you mind leaving?

SORIN: *(to MASHA)*
Masha, please ask your father to unchain that dog. It's howling all the time. My sister couldn't sleep again last night.

MASHA:
Talk to my father yourself. I'm not going to. Leave me out of it. *(to MEDVEDENKO)* Let's go.

MEDVEDENKO: *(to TREPLYOV)*
You'll let us know when the play begins, won't you? *(MASHA and MEDVEDENKO exit.)*

SORIN:
That means the dog'll be howling again all night. Well, there you are, I've never lived in the country the way I wanted. I used to get a month's vacation and I'd come here for a rest and what have you. But I'd no sooner get here than I'd be pestered with all kinds of nonsense and want to leave right away. *(laughs)* I was always glad to . . . Well, now I'm retired, I've nowhere to go, and that's that. Like it or not . . . you live . . .

YAKOV: *(to TREPLYOV)*
We're going for a swim, sir.

11

TREPLYOV:
> All right, but be back in ten minutes. *(looks at his watch)* We'll be starting soon.

YAKOV:
> Yes, sir. *(exits)*

TREPLYOV: *(looking around the stage)*
> How's this for a theatre? A curtain, two wings, and open space. No scenery. Just the lake and the horizon. We'll raise the curtain exactly at half-past eight, when the moon rises.

SORIN:
> Marvellous.

TREPLYOV:
> Of course if Nina's late, the whole effect will be ruined. She should be here by now. But her father and stepmother practically keep her prisoner, the way they watch her. *(straightens his Uncle's tie)* Your hair and beard are a mess. You should get a trim . . .

SORIN: *(combing his beard)*
> That's the tragedy of my life. Even when I was young I looked like a drunk — and that's it. Women have never loved me. *(sits down)* Why is my sister in such a foul mood?

TREPLYOV:
> Why? She's bored. *(sits down beside SORIN)* And jealous. She's got it in for me, and the play, and the performance, all because Nina's in it and she's not. She doesn't know the play but she already hates it.

SORIN: *(laughing)*
> You're just imagining that, really . . .

TREPLYOV:
> No, she's angry because Nina will get the applause

12

and not her, even on this tiny stage. *(looks at his watch)* She's a psychological case, my mother. She's gifted, intelligent, she can weep over a novel, recite all Nekrasov's[4] poems by heart, nurse the sick like an angel; but don't praise Duse[5] in front of her, uh-uh! You praise only her, write only of her, and you rave about her marvellous performance in *Camille*[6] or *The Fumes of Life*.[7] But flattery's a drug she can't get in the country, so she's bored, she's irritated. We're all her enemies — it's all our fault. Besides that she's superstitious, afraid of three candles or the number thirteen. She's stingy. She's got seventy thousand rubles in the Odessa Bank — I know for a fact. But ask for a loan and she bursts into tears.

SORIN:
You think your mother doesn't like your play and you're all upset and everything. Calm down, your mother adores you.

TREPLYOV: *(picking petals off a flower)*
She loves me, she loves me not. She loves me, she loves me not. She loves me, she loves me not. *(laughs)* You see, my mother doesn't love me. How could she? She wants to live, love, wear beautiful clothes, but here I am twenty-five years old, a constant reminder she's not young anymore. When I'm not around she's thirty-two; when I am, she's forty-three, and she hates me for that. Besides, she knows I don't recognize the theatre. She loves the theatre. She thinks she's serving humanity, Sacred Art, but to me the theatre today — it's routine, conventional. When the curtain goes up, and in artificial light we see a room with three walls, and these great geniuses, these priests of Sacred Art proceed to show us how people eat, drink, walk, make love, and wear their jackets;[8] when they try to squeeze a moral from the tritest scenes and phrases, some cozy little message anyone can under-stand and use around the house; when they serve up the same stale dish over and over, again and again, in a thousand variations, then I run and I run, the way

13

Maupassant ran from the Eiffel tower, which crushed his brain with its banality.

SORIN:

We can't do without the theatre.

TREPLYOV:

We need new forms. And if we can't find them, we'd be better off with nothing. *(looks at his watch)* I love my mother, love her very much. But her life's so stupid, always trailing after that novelist, her name bandied about in the papers. It's disgusting. Maybe I'm just selfish. I don't like having a mother who's a famous actress. I think I'd be happier if she were just an ordinary woman. Uncle, what could be more desperate, more absurd, than this? When she entertained all those celebrities, those actors and writers, I was the only nobody. And they put up with me only because I was her son. Who am I? What am I? I left university in my third year, owing to circumstances beyond our control, as they say. I have no trade, no money, and my passport reads: Kiev shopkeeper.[9] That's what my father was, besides being a famous actor. Anyway, when those celebrities patronized me with their attention, I felt they were judging me a nobody. I could read their minds, and it was humiliating . . .

SORIN:

By the way, what's he like, this novelist? I can't make him out. Never says much.

TREPLYOV:

He's intelligent, down to earth, a little melancholy. Decent enough. He's not yet forty and he's already famous. He has everything he wants . . . As for his writing, well . . . let's say it's attractive, skillful . . . but . . . after Tolstoy or Zola you don't feel like reading Trigorin.

SORIN:
Still, my boy, I love writers. There used to be two things I wanted passionately: to get married and be a writer. But nothing came of either. Yes. It must be pleasant just being a minor writer, I should think.

TREPLYOV: *(listens)*
Someone's coming . . .   *(embraces his Uncle)*   I can't live without her . . . Even the sound of her footsteps is beautiful . . . I'm insanely happy. *(hurries to meet NINA ZARECHNAYA as she enters)* My enchantress! My dream!

NINA: *(agitatedly)*
I'm not late . . . Surely I'm not late . . .

TREPLYOV: *(kissing her hands)*
No, no, no . . .

NINA:
I've been worried all day, so frightened! I was afraid father wouldn't let me come . . . But he just went out with my stepmother. The sky was red, the moon was rising, and I raced the horse . . . I raced it.   *(laughs)* Oh, I'm so happy to be here.   *(warmly shakes SORIN's hand)*

SORIN: *(laughing)*
You've been crying. I can tell from those pretty eyes . . . Tch-tch-tch! That's not good!

NINA:
Yes . . . you can see how out of breath I am. Let's hurry. I've got to leave in half an hour. I really must. And don't ask me to stay; my father doesn't know I'm here.

TREPLYOV:
It's time to start, anyway. I'll call the others.

SORIN:

> I'll go then, shall I? Right away . . .   *(He crosses right, singing.)*   "Two grenadiers to France did march . . ."[10]   *(looks back)*   One time when I began to sing like that, the public prosecutor said, "You've got a powerful voice, Your Excellency . . ." Then he thought for a moment and said, "Powerful . . . but unpleasant."   *(He exits, laughing.)*

NINA:

> My father and his wife won't let me come here. They say you're all Bohemians . . . They're afraid I'll become an actress . . . But I'm drawn to this lake like a seagull . . . My heart is full of you.   *(looks round)*

TREPLYOV:

> We're alone.

NINA:

> I think there's someone there . . .

TREPLYOV:

> There's no one.   *(kisses her)*

NINA:

> What kind of tree is that?

TREPLYOV:

> An elm.

NINA:

> Why is it so dark?

TREPLYOV:

> It's evening, everything gets dark. Don't leave early, please don't.

NINA:

> I must.

TREPLYOV:
   What if I follow you, Nina? I'll stand in the garden all
   night and watch your window.

NINA:
   No, don't. The watchman would see you, and
   Treasure would bark. He's not used to you yet.

TREPLYOV:
   I love you.

NINA:
   Ssh! . . .

TREPLYOV: *(hears footsteps)*
   Who's that? Is that you, Yakov?

YAKOV: *(behind the stage)*
   Yes, sir.

TREPLYOV:
   Take your places, it's time to start. Is the moon rising?

YAKOV:
   Yes, sir.

TREPLYOV:
   Do you have the methylated spirits? And the sulphur?
   When the red eyes appear, make sure there's a smell
   of sulphur.   *(to NINA)*   Better get ready, it's
   almost time. Are you nervous?

NINA:
   Yes, very. I'm not afraid of your mother . . . It's
   Trigorin . . . a famous writer . . . I'm terrified, I'm
   ashamed to act in front of him . . . Is he young?

TREPLYOV:
   Yes.

17

NINA:
He writes such wonderful stories!

TREPLYOV: *(coldly)*
I wouldn't know. I've never read them.

NINA:
It's hard to act in your play. There are no living
characters.

TREPLYOV:
Living characters! I have to show life as it appears in
dreams, not as it is or should be.[11]

NINA:
There's no action, it's all talk. I think a play should
have love in it . . . .

They exit behind the stage. Enter POLINA and DORN.

POLINA:
It's getting damp. Go put your rubbers on.

DORN:
I'm hot.

POLINA:
You don't take care of yourself, you're just stubborn.
You're a doctor, you know very well damp air's bad
for you, but you want to make me miserable. You
deliberately sat out on that terrace all last evening . . .

DORN: *(sings quietly)*
"Say not that youth has perished. . ."[12]

POLINA:
You were so busy talking to Madame Arkadina . . . you
didn't even notice the cold. You find her attractive,
don't you? Admit it . . .

DORN:
  I'm fifty-five.

POLINA:
  Nonsense. That's not old for a man. You're well-preserved. You're still attractive.

DORN:
  So what is it you want?

POLINA:
  You kiss the ground she walks on. All of you! Just because she's an actress.

DORN: (sings quietly)
  "Once more before thee. . ."[13] It's natural for people to fuss over actors and treat them differently from, say, merchants. That's what you call idealism.

POLINA:
  Women have always thrown themselves at you. I suppose that's idealism, too?

DORN: (shrugging his shoulders)
  What of it? There was a lot of good in what women felt for me. Mostly they loved me because I was a first-rate doctor. Ten or fifteen years ago, remember, I was the only decent obstetrician in the whole district. Besides, I've always been an honorable man.

POLINA: (gripping his hands)
  My darling!

DORN:
  Ssh. They're coming.

  *Enter IRINA ARKADINA on SORIN's arm,
  TRIGORIN,[14] SHAMRAYEV, MEDVEDENKO
  and MASHA.)*

19

SHAMRAYEV:
> She was a pure delight at the Poltava Fair in '73.
> Magnificent, just magnificent. But whatever happened
> to Chadin, the comedian pavel Semyonovich Chadin?
> He was perfection as Rasplyuyev, even better than
> Sadovsky.[15] Take my word for it, dear lady,
> perfection. Where is he now?

ARKADINA:
> You keep after me about these ancient relics. How
> should I know! *(sits down)*

SHAMRAYEV: *(sighing)*
> Pashka Chadin! We've seen the last of his kind. No,
> the theatre's not what it was, Irina Nikolayevna. In
> those days we had great oaks, now it's just stumps.

DORN:
> There aren't many brilliant actors these days, that's
> true, but the general level of acting is much higher.

SHAMRAYEV:
> I can't agree with you. However, it's a matter of taste.
> *De gustibus aut bene, aut nihil.*[16]

> *TREPLYOV enters from behind the stage.*

ARKADINA: *(to her son)*
> When does it start, my darling?

TREPLYOV:
> In a minute. Please be patient.

ARKADINA: *(reciting from Hamlet)*
> "Oh, Hamlet, speak no more;
> Thou turn'st mine eyes into my very soul;
> And there I see such black and grained spots
> As will not leave their tint."

TREPLYOV: *(paraphrasing Hamlet)*
> "Nay, but to live

In wickedness, to seek love
In the depths of sin . . ."[17]

A horn sounds behind the stage.

TREPLYOV:
Ladies and gentlemen, the play's about to start. Your
attention please. *(pause)* I shall begin. *(bangs
his stick on the ground and says loudly)* Oh, ancient
shades that drift above this lake at night, darken our
eyes with sleep and reveal in dreams what life will be
in two hundred thousand years!

SORIN:
There'll be nothing in two hundred thousand years.

TREPLYOV:
Then let them show us nothing.

ARKADINA:
Let them. We're asleep.

The curtain rises, revealing the lake in the background.
The moon is above the horizon, reflected in the water.
NINA, all in white, sits on a boulder.)

NINA:
Men, lions, eagles, and partridges, antlered deer,
geese, spiders, the silent fish of the deep, starfish, and
creatures invisible to the eye — these and all life have
run their melancholy cycle and are no more . . .
Thousands of centuries have passed since there was life
on earth. In vain now does the pale moon light her
lamp. The cranes no longer wake and cry in the
meadows, and the May beetles are silent in the lime
groves. Cold, cold, cold. Empty, empty, empty.
Terrible, terrible, terrible. *(pause)* Living
bodies have turned to dust. Eternal Matter has
transformed them into stones, water, clouds, and all
their souls have merged into one. I am that World
Soul . . . I. I contain the soul of Alexander the

21

Great, Caesar, Shakespeare, Napoleon, and the lowest
leech. In me the mind of man merges with the
instincts of animals. I remember all, all, and relive
each life within me.   *(Will-o'-the-wisps appear.)*

ARKADINA: *(in a whisper)*
This is like the Decadents.[18]

TREPLYOV: *(imploringly and reproachfully)*
Mama!

NINA:
I am alone. Once in a hundred years I open my lips to
speak, and in this void my sad echo goes unheard . . .
And you, pale lights, you hear me not . . . You are
born at dawn in the putrid marsh, and you wander
until sunrise, without thought, without will, without
the pulse of life. Fearing lest life should start again in
you, the Devil, father of Eternal Matter, causes your
atoms to change each instant, as in stones and water,
and you are in ceaseless flux. Within the universe only
I, the World Soul, remain unchanged and eternal.
(pause)   I am like a prisoner cast into a deep, empty
well. I know not where I am nor what awaits me. One
thing only is not hidden from me: that in the fierce
relentless struggle with the Devil, the principle of
material force, I am destined to triumph. Then Matter
and Spirit will merge in perfect harmony and usher in
the reign of Universal Will. But that is not to be until
a long series of millennia have passed, and the Moon,
shining Sirius, and the Earth have turned to dust . . .
Until then, horror, horror, horror . . .   *(Pause.)*

Two red eyes appear against the background of the lake.

NINA:
Behold, my powerful enemy, the Devil, approaches. I
see his fearsome, blood-red eyes . . .

ARKADINA:
I smell sulphur. Is that necessary?

22

TREPLYOV:
Yes.

ARKADINA: *(laughing)*
Oh, a stage effect.

TREPLYOV:
Mama!

NINA:
But without man he is restless . . .

POLINA: *(to DORN)*
You've taken your hat off. Put it on, you'll catch cold.

ARKADINA:
The doctor's taken his hat off to the Devil, the father
of Eternal Matter.

TREPLYOV: *(blows up)*
That's it! The play's over! Curtain!

ARKADINA:
Why are you angry?

TREPLYOV:
Enough! Curtain!   *(The curtain falls.)*   Forgive
me. I forgot that only a chosen few can write and act.
I was infringing on a monopoly. I . . . I . . .   *(Unable
to finish, he makes a gesture of frustration and exits left.)*

ARKADINA:
What's wrong with him?

SORIN:
Irina, my dear, that's no way to treat a young man's
pride.

ARKADINA:
What did I say?

SORIN:
    You hurt his feelings.

ARKADINA:
    But he told us beforehand it was all a joke, so that's
    how I took it.

SORIN:
    Still. . .

ARKADINA:
    And now it seems he's written a masterpiece! Well, do
    tell! So it wasn't a joke after all. He put this thing on
    and choked us all with sulphur just to show us how to
    write and act . . . Well, that's the limit. I'm sick to
    death of these constant digs and outbursts. He's an
    unruly, conceited boy.

SORIN:
    He only wanted to please you.

ARKADINA:
    Is that a fact? Then why didn't he choose an ordinary
    play instead of forcing us to listen to his Decadent
    nonsense? I can listen to rubbish. I don't mind
    listening to it so long as I'm not asked to take it
    seriously. But here you have new forms, a new Epoch
    in Art. In my opinion it's not new forms we've
    witnessed, but simply bad character.

TRIGORIN:
    Everyone writes as he wishes and as he can.

ARKADINA:
    Well, let him write as he wishes and as he can, but let
    him leave me in peace.

DORN:
    Jupiter, thou art angry . . .

ARKADINA:
I'm not Jupiter. I'm a woman. *(lights a cigarette)* I'm not angry. I'm just annoyed to see a young man wasting his time. I didn't mean to hurt his feelings.

MEDVEDENKO:
There are no grounds for separating matter from spirit, because spirit itself may be composed of material atoms. *(eagerly, to TRIGORIN)* You know, somebody ought to write a play about schoolmasters. It's a hard, hard life.

ARKADINA:
True enough, but let's not talk about plays or atoms. It's such a glorious evening! Listen . . . Is that singing? *(listens)* How lovely!

POLINA:
It's on the other shore. *(pause)*

ARKADINA: *(to TRIGORIN)*
Sit beside me. You know, ten or fifteen years ago there was music and singing by this lake almost every night. There were six estates on the shore, and I can remember the laughter, the noise, the shooting, and all the love affairs. So many love affairs . . . and the *jeune premier*[19] and the idol of all six estates was our friend here — let me present — *(nods towards DORN)* Doctor Yevgeny Sergeyevich. He's charming now, but in those days he was irresistible. My conscience is starting to bother me. Why did I hurt my poor boy? I'm worried. *(loudly)* Kostya! Son! Kostya!

MASHA:
I'll go look for him.

ARKADINA:
Would you, darling?

25

MASHA: *(crossing left, calling)*
    Yoo-hoo! Constantine! Yoo-hoo!   *(exits)*

NINA: *(entering from behind the stage)*
    I guess we're not going on, so I may as well come out.
    Good evening.   *(kisses IRINA and POLINA)*

SORIN:
    Bravo! Bravo!

ARKADINA:
    Bravo, bravo! You were enchanting. With your looks
    and that lovely voice it would be a crime to bury
    yourself in the country. You must have talent, do you
    hear? You owe it to yourself to go on the stage.

NINA:
    Oh, that's my dream!   *(sighs)*   But it'll never
    happen.

ARKADINA:
    Who knows? Now, allow me to present Boris
    Alekseyevich Trigorin.

NINA:
    Oh, I'm so pleased . . .   *(embarrassed)*   I always
    read you . . .

ARKADINA: *(sitting NINA beside her)*
    Don't be shy, darling. He may be a famous writer,
    but he's simple at heart. Look, he's embarrassed, too.

DORN:
    I wonder if we could raise the curtain now. It's eerie
    like that.

SHAMRAYEV: *(loudly)*
    Yakov, lad, get that curtain up!

        The curtain goes up.

NINA: *(to TRIGORIN)*
It's a strange play, isn't it?

TRIGORIN:
I didn't understand a word. Still, I enjoyed it. You were
very sincere, and the set was lovely. *(pause)* There
must be a lot of fish in this lake.

NINA:
Yes.

TRIGORIN:
I love fishing. There's nothing finer than to sit on a
bank in the evening, watching a float.

NINA:
For someone who's experienced the joy of creation I'd
have thought no other pleasure could exist.

ARKADINA: *(laughing)*
Don't talk like that. He falls apart when he gets a
compliment.

SHAMRAYEV:
I remember one evening at the Moscow Opera when
the famous Silva took a low C. It so happened that the
bass from our church choir was sitting in the gallery,
and all of a sudden — you can imagine our amazement —
we heard, "Bravo, Silva!" but a whole octave lower.
Like this. *(in a deep bass)* "Bravo, Silva!"[20]
You could hear a pin drop.

Pause.

DORN:
The angel of silence just flew over.[21]

NINA:
Well, I must go now. Goodbye.

ARKADINA:
   What? So early? We won't hear of it.

NINA:
   Father'll be waiting.

ARKADINA:
   What a man, really . . .   *(they kiss)*   Well, it
   can't be helped. But it's a shame to see you go.

NINA:
   If you only knew how I hate to.

ARKADINA:
   Someone should see you home, my pet.

NINA: *(frightened)*
   Oh, no, no!

SORIN: *(imploringly)*
   Please stay!

NINA:
   I can't, Peter Nikolayevich.

SORIN:
   Stay an hour, that's all. Come now, really . . .

NINA: *(considering a moment, in tears)*
   I can't!   *(shakes his hand and hurries off)*

ARKADINA:
   Poor child. They say when her mother died she left the
   entire fortune to the husband, every kopeck. And now
   she has nothing because he's willed it all to the second
   wife. It's shocking.

DORN:
   Yes, the man's a swine, I'll grant him that.

SORIN: *(rubbing his hands to warm them)*
Let's go inside. It's getting damp. My legs are aching.

ARKADINA:
They're so stiff you can hardly walk. Come along, you poor old man. *(takes his arm)*

SHAMRAYEV:: *(offering his arm to his wife)*
Madame?

SORIN:
There's that dog again. *(to SHAMRAYEV)* Be good enough, Shamrayev, to have it unchained.

SHAMRAYEV:
Can't be done, Peter Nikolayevich. Thieves will get in the barn and steal the millet. *(to MEDVEDENKO, who walks beside him)* That's right, a whole octave lower. "Bravo, Silva!" And no concert singer, mind you, just ordinary church choir.

MEDVEDENKO:
What would he earn, a chorister? *(All except DORN exit.)*

DORN: *(alone)*
I don't know. Maybe I'm no judge, or maybe I'm crazy, but I liked that play. It had something. When the girl spoke of solitude and later when the Devil's red eyes appeared, I could feel my hands trembling. It was all so fresh and naive . . . Here he comes now. I'd like to say something nice. *(enter TREPLYOV)*

TREPLYOV:
They've all gone.

DORN:
I'm here.

TREPLYOV:

Masha's been all over the park, hunting for me. Insufferable creature.

DORN:

I admired your play very much. Constantine Gavrilovich. It's strange somehow, and I don't know the ending, but it made a strong impression. You've got a real talent. You must keep writing. *(TREPLYOV shakes his hand and grips him impulsively.)* Whew, how nervous. Tears in his eyes . . . What is it I wanted to say? . . . You took your subject from the realm of abstract ideas, and that's right. A work of art should express a great idea. Without seriousness, there's no beauty. How pale you are.

TREPLYOV:

So you think . . . I should keep writing?

DORN:

Yes . . . but express only what's important and universal. You know I've lived a full and varied life, and I've enjoyed it. I'm content. But if I'd ever felt the ecstasy artists must feel while creating, I think I'd forsake this earthly shell and all its trappings, and soar off into the heights.

TREPLYOV:

Excuse me, but where's Nina?

DORN:

One more point. A work of art should have a clear, definite idea. You must know why you're writing. If you take the literary road with no definite aim, you'll get lost and your talent will destroy you.

TREPLYOV: *(impatiently)*
Where's Nina?

DORN:

She's gone home.

TREPLYOV: *(in despair)*
    What will I do? I want to see her . . . I must see
    her . . . I'm going . . .

    MASHA enters.

DORN: *(to TREPLYOV)*
    Calm down, my friend.

TREPLYOV:
    I'm still going. I must.

MASHA:
    Constantine Gavrilovich, come inside. Your mother
    wants you. She's worried.

TREPLYOV:
    Tell her I've gone. And please, all of you, just leave
    me alone! Stop following me around!

DORN:
    Come, now, my boy . . . you mustn't act like
    this . . . It's not right.

TREPLYOV: *(moved)*
    Goodbye, Doctor. And thank you . . .   *(exits)*

DORN: *(sighing)*
    Youth, youth!

MASHA:
    When they can't think of anything else, people say
    "Youth, youth . . ."   *(takes a pinch of snuff)*

DORN: *(takes the snuffbox from her and flings it into the
    bushes)*
    Disgusting habit!   *(pause)*   Someone's playing
    the piano. We'd better go in.

MASHA:
    No, wait.

DORN:

> What is it?

MASHA:

> I want to try and tell you. I want to talk . . . *(upset)*
> I don't love my father . . . but I'm fond of you.
> Somehow I feel with my whole soul that you're close
> to me . . . Help me. Help me or I'll do something
> stupid. I'll make a mockery of my life, I'll ruin
> it . . . I can't go on . . .

DORN:

> What is it? Help you how?

MASHA:

> I'm suffering. Nobody, nobody knows how I
> suffer! *(rests her head on his chest, softly)* I love
> Constantine.

DORN:

> How nervous they all are! So high-strung! And so
> much love . . . O magic lake! *(tenderly)* But
> what can I do, my child? What? What?

> *Curtain*

ACT TWO

*The croquet lawn. In the background, right, is the house,
with a large terrace. The lake is left, sparkling with
sunlight. Flower beds. It is noon and hot. ARKADINA,
DORN, and MASHA are sitting on a bench near the
lawn in the shade of an old lime tree. DORN has an
open book on his lap.*

ARKADINA: *(to MASHA)*
Let's stand up.   *(They both rise.)*   Side by side.
You're twenty-two and I'm twice that, almost.
Yevgeny Sergeyevich, which of us looks younger?

DORN:
You, of course.

ARKADINA:
There . . . And why's that? Because I work, I feel,
I'm always on the go. But you, you're stuck in the
same spot all the time, you don't live . . . I make it a
rule never to think of the future. I never dwell on old
age or death. What will be, will be.

MASHA:
But I feel I was born so long ago; and I'm dragging
my life behind me like an endless train . . . and often I
just don't want to live.   *(sits down)*   That's all
rubbish of course. I ought to shake myself, snap out of it.

33

DORN: *(sings quietly)*
"Tell her, pretty flowers . . ."²²

ARKADINA:
Besides, I'm as correct as an Englishman. I keep
myself in trim, and my hair and dress are always
comme il faut. Would I let myself be seen outside the
house, even in the garden, in a dressing gown or my
hair not done? Never. That's why I've kept my looks.
I've never been slovenly, never let myself go like
some . . .   *(Hands on hips, she walks up and down the
lawn.)*   There. You see? Light as a bird. I could
play a girl of fifteen.

DORN:
Mmmmm . . . well . . . I'll go on reading, shall
I?   *(picks up the book)*   We stopped at the corn
merchant and the rats . . .

ARKADINA:
Yes, the rats. Go on.   *(sits)*   No, let me have it,
I'll read. It's my turn.   *(takes the book and looks for
the place)*   The rats . . . Here we are . . .   *(reads)*
"And of course it's as dangerous for society people to
pamper novelists and lure them into their homes as it
is for corn merchants to breed rats in their granaries.
And yet novelists are much in demand. So when a
woman has chosen the writer she wants to capture, she
besieges him with compliments, flattery and
favours . . ." Well, that may be true of the French,
but with us there's nothing like that, no plan of action.
With us, you see, a woman is usually head over heels
in love with a writer before she sets out to capture
him. You don't have to go very far. Take me and
Trigorin . . .

*Enter SORIN, leaning on his walking stick, with
NINA at his side. MEDVEDENKO follows pushing
an empty wheelchair.*

34

SORIN: *(fondly, as to a child)*
Is that so? We've had a nice surprise, have we? We're happy today, are we? *(to his sister)* We've had a nice surprise. Father and stepmother went to Tver, and we're free for three whole days.

NINA: *(sits next to ARKADINA and embraces her)*
I'm so happy! I'm all yours now.

SORIN: *(sitting down in the wheelchair)*
She looks so lovely today.

ARKADINA:
Yes, elegant, interesting . . . That's a clever girl. *(kisses NINA)* But we mustn't praise her too much, it's bad luck. Where's Boris Alekseyevich?

NINA:
He's down at the bathhouse, fishing.

ARKADINA:
You'd think he'd get bored with it! *(She goes back to the book.)*

NINA:
What's that?

ARKADINA:
Maupassant's *Sur l'eau*,[23] my darling. *(reads a few lines to herself)* Oh, well, the rest is dull, it's just not true. *(shuts the book)* I'm troubled. Tell me, what is it with my son? Why's he so depressed, so sombre? He spends whole days on the lake, I hardly ever see him.

MASHA:
His soul is troubled. *(to NINA timidly)* Please, would you recite from his play?

NINA: *(shrugging)*
You really want me to? It's so uninteresting!

MASHA: *(with restrained eagerness)*
His eyes burn when he recites, and his face grows
pale. He has a beautiful sad voice and the look of a
poet.

SORIN snores.

DORN:
Sweet dreams!

ARKADINA: *(to SORIN)*
Petrusha!

SORIN:
Uh?

ARKADINA:
You asleep?

SORIN:
Not in the least.   *(pause)*

ARKADINA:
You're not taking care of yourself, brother. That's not
right.

SORIN:
I'd be glad to take care of myself, but the doctor here
won't give me a cure.

DORN:
A cure at sixty!

SORIN:
Even at sixty a man wants to live.

DORN: *(irritably)*
Oh? Then take your valerian drops.

ARKADINA:
I think it would do him good to go to a spa.

DORN:
Well, he could go to a spa. He could also not go.

ARKADINA:
Understand that, if you can.

DORN:
Nothing to understsand. It's quite clear.   *(pause)*

MEDVEDENKO:
Peter Nikolayevich should give up smoking.

SORIN:
Nonsense.

DORN:
No, it's not nonsense. Wine and tobacco are depersonalizing. After a cigar or vodka, you're not Peter Nikolayevich, you're Peter Nikolayevich plus somebody else. Your ego disintegrates and you think of yourself in the third person.

SORIN: *(laughs)*
It's all right for you to talk, you've lived your life. But what about me? I've worked for the Department of Justice twenty-eight years, but I've never really lived, never experienced anything, if you know what I mean. So it's understandable, I want to live. You've had your fill of life, you don't care anymore, so you can afford to philosophize. But I want to live, so I drink sherry and smoke cigars after dinner and what have you. And that's that.

DORN:
Life should be taken seriously. To look for cures at sixty and regret you missed the pleasures of youth — that's just fatuous, if you don't mind my saying so.

MASHA: *(rises)*
It must be time for lunch. *(walking languidly and with effort)* My foot's gone to sleep . . . *(exits)*

DORN:
She'll belt back a few before lunch.

SORIN:
The poor girl's so unhappy.

DORN:
Nonsense, Your Excellency.

SORIN:
Spoken like a man who's had his fill.

ARKADINA:
Oh, what can be more boring that this charming country boredom! The heat, the quiet, the idleness, the philosophizing . . . It's good to be with you, my friends, it's pleasant to hear you talk, but . . . I'd rather be in my hotel room, studying a part.

NINA: *(rapturously)*
Oh, yes! I understand.

SORIN:
Of course it's better in town. You sit in your study, no one gets in unannounced, and there's a telephone . . . cabbies in the street and so on . . .

DORN: *(sings quietly)*
"Tell her, pretty flowers . . ."

Enter SHAMRAYEV followed by POLINA.

SHAMRAYEV:
Here we are. Good morning! *(kisses ARKADINA's hand, then NINA's)* Wonderful to see you looking so well. *(to ARKADINA)* My wife tells me you two are planning to drive into town today. Is that so?

ARKADINA:
Yes, we're planning to.

SHAMRAYEV:
Hm . . . That's marvellous, but how will you manage that, dear lady? We're carting the rye today, all the men are busy. And what horses would you take, may I ask?

ARKADINA:
What horses? How should I know what horses?

SORIN:
We have carriage horses.

SHAMRAYEV: *(angrily)*
Carriage horses? And where do I get the harness? Where do I get the harness? This is amazing! It's beyond me! My dear lady! Forgive me, I worship your talent, I'd gladly give you ten years of my life, but I can't give you horses!

ARKADINA:
And what if I have to go? A fine state of affairs!

SHAMRAYEV:
Dear lady! You have no idea what it means to run a farm![24]

ARKADINA: *(angrily)*
As you are always so quick to remind me! In that case I'm leaving for Moscow at once. Hire horses for me in the village, or I'll walk to the station!

SHAMRAYEV: *(angrily)*
In that case I resign! Find yourself another manager! *(exits)*

ARKADINA:
Every summer it's like this. Every summer they insult me! I won't set foot in this place again!

*ARKADINA exits, left, in the direction of the
bathhouse. A moment later she is seen entering the house,
followed by TRIGORIN with fishing rods and a pail.*

SORIN: *(angrily)*
The insolence! What in the hell's going on! I'm sick of
it, and that's that. Bring all the horses here right this
minute!

NINA: *(to POLINA)*
To refuse a famous actress like Irina Nikolayevna!
Surely anything she fancies — no matter how small —
is more important than your farming? It's simply
incredible!

POLINA: *(in despair)*
What can I do? Put yourself in my place. What can I
do?

SORIN: *(to NINA)*
Let's go find my sister . . . We'll all beg her to stay.
All right?   *(looking in the direction SHAMRAYEV
took)*   Impossible man! Tyrant!

NINA: *(prevents his rising)*
Sit, sit . . . We'll wheel you . . .   *(She and
MEDVEDENKO push the wheelchair.)*   Oh, this is
dreadful!

SORIN:
Yes, yes, it's dreadful! But he won't leave. I'll speak
to him right away.

They go out. DORN and POLINA remain.

DORN:
People are boring. That husband of yours should be
tossed out by the scruff of the neck, but that old
woman, Peter Nikolayevich, and his sister will
apologize. You'll see!

POLINA:

> He's even put the carriage horses in the fields. Not a
> day goes by without a quarrel. If you only knew how
> it all upsets me! It makes me ill. Look how I'm
> trembling . . . I can't stand his coarseness. *(imploringly)*
> Yevgeny, my darling, light of my eyes, let me live with
> you . . . Our time's passing, we're not young
> anymore. If we could only stop hiding things, stop
> lying, at least for what's left of our lives . . . *(pause)*

DORN:

> I'm fifty-five. It's a bit late to change my life.

POLINA:

> I know . . . There are other women besides me. You
> can't live with us all. I understand. Forgive me, I've
> bored you.

> *NINA appears near the house, picking flowers.*

DORN:

> No, not at all.

POLINA:

> I'm sick with jealousy. Of course, you're a doctor, you
> can't avoid women. I understand . . .

DORN: *(to NINA as she approaches)*
> What's happening?

NINA:

> Irina Nikolayevna's crying and Peter Nikolayevich is
> having an asthma attack.

DORN: *(getting up)*
> I'd better give them both valerian drops.

NINA: *(gives him the flowers)*
> May I?

DORN:
Merci bien.   *(goes towards the house)*

POLINA: *(going with him)*
What lovely flowers!   *(near the house, in a low
voice)*   Give me those flowers! Give me those
flowers!

> *He hands her the flowers. She tears them to pieces and
> throws them away. They both enter the house.*

NINA: *(alone)*
How strange to see a famous actress cry, and over
such a little thing! And isn't it strange that a famous
writer who's adored by the public, written up in all the
papers, his portraits sold in shop windows, his books
published in foreign languages . . . isn't it strange he
would spend the whole day fishing and be delighted
just to catch two chub? I though famous people were
proud and aloof, and despised the public. I thought
they used their fame to get back at society for making
so much of birth and money. But here they are crying
or fishing, playing cards, laughing, losing their tempers,
just like everyone else . . .

TREPLYOV: *(entering hatless with a gun and a dead
seagull)* [25]
Are you alone? ·

NINA:
Yes.

> *TREPLYOV lays the seagull at her feet.*

NINA:
What does that mean?

TREPLYOV:
I did a shamefull thing today. I killed this seagull. I
lay it at your feet.

42

NINA:
What's wrong with you? *(picks up the seagull and looks at it)*

TREPLYOV: *(pause)*
I'll soon end my own life the same way.

NINA:
I don't recognize you.

TREPLYOV:
Yes, but who changed first, you or me? Your eyes are cold. My presence embarrasses you.

NINA:
You've been irritable lately. You don't make sense, you talk in symbols. And this seagull's a symbol, too, I suppose. Forgive me, but I don't understand . . . *(lays the seagull on the bench)*   I'm too simple to understand you.

TREPLYOV:
It all started that evening my play was such a stupid failure. Women never forgive failure. I've burnt it all, every last scrap. If you only knew how unhappy I am. Your coldness terrifies me, it's incredible! It's as though I woke up and found this lake had suddenly dried up or vanished into the earth. You say you're too simple to understand me. But what's there to understand? You didn't like my play, you despise my inspiration. You think I'm mediocre, insignificant like hundreds of others . . .   *(stamping his foot)*   Oh, I understand it all right. I understand! It's like a nail in my brain. Damn it and damn my pride that sucks my lifeblood like a serpent . . .   *(He sees TRIGORIN, who enters reading a book.)*   Here comes the real genius, like Hamlet, and with a book, too.   *(mimicking)* "Words, words, words . . ." He's not even close, the sun, but already you're smiling. Your eyes are melting in his rays. I won't stand in your way.   *(He exits.)*

43

TRIGORIN: *(jotting in a notebook)*
Takes snuff and drinks vodka . . . Always wears black. The schoolmaster in love with her . . .

NINA:
Good morning, Boris Alekseyevich!

TRIGORIN:
Good morning. Things took an unexpected turn, so it looks like we're leaving today. We're not likely to meet again, you and I. That's too bad. I don't often meet young girls, young *and* interesting. I've forgotten what it's like to be eighteen or nineteen, can't picture it clearly. That's why the girls in my stories are so unconvincing. I'd like to be in your shoes for just one hour, to find out how you think, what makes you tick.

NINA:
And I'd like to be in your shoes.

TRIGORIN:
Why?

NINA:
To find out how it feels to be a famous, gifted writer. What's it like to be famous? How does it feel?

TRIGORIN:
How? No way in particular. I've never thought about it.   *(He thinks.)*   It's either one of two things: either I'm not as famous as you think or else it's something you just don't feel.

NINA:
But what happens when you read about yourself in the newspapers?

TRIGORIN:
When they praise you it's pleasant. When they attack you, you're down for a day or two.

NINA:

What a wonderful life! If you only knew how I envy you! People's lots are so different. Some barely drag out their dull, obscure lives. They're all alike, all miserable. But others . . . like you, for instance, you're one in a million. Your life is bright, interesting, full of meaning. You're happy . . .

TRIGORIN:

I am? *(shrugs his shoulders)* Hm . . . You speak of fame, happiness, a bright, interesting life. I'm sorry, but all those fine words mean about as much to me as marmalade, which I never eat. You're very young and very kind.

NINA:

Your life is beautiful!

TRIGORIN:

What's so good about it? *(looks at his watch)* I must get to work. Excuse me, I don't have time . . . *(laughs)* You've stepped on my favorite corn, as they say, and now I'm excited and a little cross. But all right, let's talk. Let's talk about my beautiful, bright life . . . Well, where'll we start? *(thinks for a moment)* You know, sometimes one gets obsessed with a fixed idea. The moon, for example. Day and night you think of nothing but the moon. Well, I have my own moon. Day and night I'm obsessed with one thought: I must write, I must write, I must . . . I've barely finished one story when I'm driven to write another, then a third, then a fourth . . . I write incessantly, furiously, and I cannot do otherwise. What is beautiful and bright about that, I ask you? It's a cruel life! Here I am with you, I'm excited, yet every minute I'm thinking that the story I haven't finished is waiting for me. I notice that cloud up there, shaped like a grand piano, and I make a mental note to put that in a story. "A cloud passed, shaped like a grand piano." A scent of heliotrope. I quickly make a note: "sickly odour, flowers the colour of a widow's dress, use in description of a summer evening." I pounce on every sentence, every word you and I say, and store it away for future use. It might come in handy. When I finish a work, I rush to the theatre or go fishing, hoping to relax and forget. But oh no. An iron ball is already turning in my brain — a new idea, and already it's pulling me back to the desk, and again I have to hurry to write and write. And it's always like that, always. And there's no rest for me, from myself, and I feel I'm devouring my own life; that to give honey to people I don't even know I rob my best flowers of their pollen, tear up the flowers and trample on the roots. Am I not crazy? Do you think my friends and acquaintances treat me like a sane person? "What're you writing now? What's in store for us next?" It's the same thing over and over and it seems to me that all this attention, this praise, this ecstasy — it's just a lie, they're deceiving me like an invalid, and sometimes I'm afraid they'll creep up on me from behind and cart me off to the madhouse like Gogol's Poprishchin.[26] And in those first years, my young, best years, when I was just starting out, writing was always a torment. A beginning writer feels clumsy, awkward, superfluous, especially when he's had no luck. His nerves are shot. He can't keep away from people in the arts, though no one knows him or takes any notice of him, and he's afraid to look them straight in the eye, like a passionate gambler who hasn't any money. I'd never seen my readers, but for some reason I imagined them hostile, and suspicious. I was afraid of the public, terrified, and whenever I had a new play produced, I'd feel all the brunettes in the audience were hostile and all the blondes coldly indifferent. Oh, it was awful! It was torment!

NINA:
But what about inspiration and the process of creation? Don't they give you exalted happy moments?

TRIGORIN:
Yes. I enjoy writing and I enjoy reading the proofs,

46

but . . . the minute it's published I can't stand it. I see it's all wrong, a mistake, it should never have been written, and I'm annoyed, I feel rotten inside . . . *(laughs)*   Then the public reads it and says: "Yes, charming, talented . . . charming, but a far cry from Tolstoy." Or: "A very fine piece of work, but Turgenev's *Fathers and Sons* is better." And that's what it'll be to my dying day, talented and charming, charming and talented — nothing more. And when I'm dead, my friends will pass my grave and say: "Here lies Trigorin, a good writer, but not as good as Turgenev."

NINA:

I'm sorry, but I refuse to accept that. You're just spoiled by success.

TRIGORIN:

What success? I've never been satisfied. I don't like myself as a writer. And the worst of it is I work in a sort of daze and most of the time I don't understand what I write . . . I love this lake, the trees, the sky. I have a feeling for nature. It arouses such a passion in me that I can't help but write. But I'm not just a painter of landscapes, I'm a citizen, too. I love my country and its people. As a writer I feel I've a duty to write about the people, their sufferings, their future, about science, the rights of man and so on, and so forth. And I write about everything, everything, always in a hurry, driven on, criticized from all sides. I rush from side to side like a fox with the hounds at his heels. I see life and science forging further and further ahead, while I fall farther and farther behind, like a peasant who's just missed his train. And in the end I feel I can only write landscapes and everything else is false, false to the very core.[27]

NINA:

You're overworked. You don't have time to recognize your own importance, not that you want to. You may not be satisfied with yourself, but for others you're

47

great and wonderful! If I were a writer like you, I'd give my whole life to the public, but I'd know they could be only happy rising to my level. And they'd draw me along in a chariot.

TRIGORIN:
Mmmm . . . in a chariot . . . What am I, Agamemnon? *(They both smile.)*

NINA:
I'd endure anything for the joy of being a writer or an actress. My family could disown me, I'd face poverty, disappointment, I'd live in a garret and eat black bread. I'd suffer from knowing my own limitations, but in return for all that I'd demand fame . . . real resounding fame . . .   *(covers her face with her hands)*   Oh, my head's spinning . . . Oof!

ARKADINA: *(from the house)*
Boris Alekseyevich!

TRIGORIN:
They're calling me . . . To pack, I suppose. I don't feel like leaving.   *(looks at the lake)*   Look . . . what a paradise! Wonderful!

NINA:
See that estate on the far shore?

TRIGORIN:
Yes.

NINA:
It belonged to my mother. I was born there. I've lived all my life by this lake. I know every island on it.

TRIGORIN:
It's a lovely place.   *(notices the seagull)*   What's this?

NINA:
A seagull. Constantine shot it.

TRIGORIN:
A beautiful bird. Really, I don't feel like leaving. Try and persuade Irina Nikolayevna to stay.   *(makes a note in his book)*

NINA:
What are you writing?

TRIGORIN:
Just a note . . . Had an idea . . .   *(puts the notebook away)*   An idea for a short story: a young girl like yourself has lived all her life by a lake. She loves the lake like a seagull, and she's happy and free like a seagull. But a man happens along, sees her, and out of nothing better to do, destroys her like this seagull.

Pause. ARKADINA appears in the window.

ARKADINA:
Boris Alekseyevich, where are you?

TRIGORIN:
I'm coming.   *(He goes, then looks back at NINA. At the window to ARKADINA)*   What is it?

ARKADINA:
We're staying.

TRIGORIN enters the house.

NINA: *(Moves to the front of the stage. After a moment's thought)*
It's a dream!

Curtain

ACT THREE

The dining room in SORIN's house. Doors right and left. A sideboard and medicine cupboard. A table in the middle of the room. A trunk and hatboxes; signs of impending departure. TRIGORIN is eating lunch. MASHA stands by the table.

MASHA:

I'm telling you all this because you're a writer. You might be able to use it. Honestly, if he'd seriously wounded himself I couldn't have lived another minute. Still, I've got courage. I've made up my mind. I'll tear this love out of my heart, tear it out by the roots.

TRIGORIN:

And how will you do that?

MASHA:

I'm getting married. To Medvedenko.

TRIGORIN:

The schoolmaster?

MASHA:

Yes.

TRIGORIN:

I don't see the need for that.

MASHA:

> To love without hope, to wait whole years for some-
> thing . . . Once I get married there won't be time for
> love. New cares'll drown out the old. And anyway,
> you know, it'll be a change. Should we have another?

TRIGORIN:

> Aren't you overdoing it?

MASHA:

> Oh, come on. *(pours two shots)* Don't look at
> me like that. Women drink more than you think. But
> only a few drink openly like me. Most do it in secret.
> Yes, they do. And it's always vodka or brandy. *(clinks
> glasses)* Here's to you. You're nice. I'm sorry you're
> leaving. *(They drink.)*

TRIGORIN:

> I don't want to go myself.

MASHA:

> Then why not ask her to stay?

TRIGORIN:

> No, she won't stay now. Her son's being very tactless.
> first he tries to shoot himself and now I gather he's
> going to challenge me to a duel. What for? He sulks,
> snorts, preaches new art forms . . . But really, there's
> room for everything — the old and the new. Why
> crowd each other?

MASHA:

> Well, there's jealousy. But that's none of my business.

> *Pause. YAKOV crosses right with a suitcase. NINA
> enters and stands by the window.*

MASHA:

> My schoolmaster's not all that bright, but he's kind,
> and poor, and he loves me very much. I'm sorry for
> him. And I'm sorry for his old mother. Well, I wish

51

you all the best. Don't think badly of me. *(shakes his hand warmly)* Thanks for your interest in me. Send me your books and don't forget to autograph them. Only don't write "esteemed lady." Just: "To Masha, who doesn't know where she comes from, or what she's living for." Goodbye! *(exits)*

NINA: *(holding out her clenched fist to TRIGORIN)*
Odd or even?

TRIGORIN:
Even.

NINA: *(sighing)*
Wrong. There's only one pea in my hand. I was trying to tell my fortune: do I go on the stage or not? I wish someone would advise me.

TRIGORIN:
No one can advise you on that. *(pause)*

NINA:
We're parting and . . . we may never see each other again. Please take this little medallion to remember me by. I had your initials engraved on it . . . and on the other side, the title of your book: *Days and Nights.*

TRIGORIN:
How charming! *(kisses the medallion)* A lovely gift!

NINA:
Think of me sometimes.

TRIGORIN:
I'll think of you. I'll think of you as you were on that sunny day. Remember? A week ago when you wore that light dress . . . We talked . . . and there was a white seagull lying on the bench.

NINA: *(pensively)*
Yes, the seagull . . .   *(pause)*   We can't talk any
more, someone's coming . . . Before you go, give me
two minutes, please! . . .

*NINA exits left as ARKADINA enters right with
SORIN, who wears a frock coat with decorations.*[28]
YAKOV follows, busy with the packing.

ARKADINA:
Stay home, old man. With your rheumatism, it's not
wise to be running about.   *(to TRIGORIN)*   Who
was that? Nina?

TRIGORIN:
Yes.

ARKADINA:
Pardon. We're intruding . . .   *(sits down)*   I think
everything's packed. I'm exhausted.

TRIGORIN: *(reading the inscription on the medallion)*
Days and Nights, page 121, lines 11 and 12.

YAKOV: *(clearing the table)*
Should I pack your fishing rods, too, sir?

TRIGORIN:
Yes, I'll want them again. But the books you can give
away.

YAKOV:
Yes, sir.

TRIGORIN: *(to himself)*
Page 121, lines 11 and 12. What are those lines?   *(to
ARKADINA)*   Do you have my books in the house?

ARKADINA:
Yes, in my brother's study, the corner bookcase.

TRIGORIN:
Page 121 . . .   *(exits)*

ARKADINA:
Really, Petrusha, you ought to stay home.

SORIN:
You're going away. It'll be dreary here without you.

ARKADINA:
And in town?

SORIN:
It's nothing special, but still.   *(laughs)*   They'll be laying the foundation stone for the Country Hall and that sort of thing . . . I'd like to leap out of this fishpond, just for an hour or two. I've been lying around too long, like an old cigarette holder. I've ordered the horses for one o'clock, so we'll leave at the same time.

ARKADINA: *(pause)*
Well, live here, don't get bored or catch cold. Look after my son. Take care of him. Give him guidance. *(pause)*   Here I'm going away, I'll never know why Constantine tried to shoot himself. I think the main reason was jealousy, so the sooner I take Trigorin away the better.

SORIN:
How can I say it? There were other reasons too. It's understandable; a young man, intelligent, lives in the country, in a backwater, no money, no position, no future. Nothing to keep him busy. Ashamed and afraid of his idleness. I love him a great deal and he's very attached to me, but no matter what, he still feels like an outsider, a sponger, a poor relation; it's understandable, his pride . . . .

ARKADINA:
He's such a grief to me!   *(thinks)*   Maybe he should get a job in the civil service or something . . .

54

SORIN: *(whistles; then hesitantly)*
It seems to me, the best thing would be, if you
would . . . give him a little money. In the first place,
he ought to be able to dress like a human being and so
on. Look at him, he's worn that same wretched jacket
for three years, he has no overcoat . . . *(laughs)*
And it wouldn't hurt the boy to have a little fun . . .
He might go abroad . . . It doesn't cost much, really.

ARKADINA:
Well . . . I could manage a suit, maybe, but as for
going abroad . . . No, right now I can't even manage
the suit. *(firmly)* I haven't any money!
(SORIN laughs.) I haven't!

SORIN: *(whistles)*
Of course, my dear. Forgive me, don't be angry. I
believe you . . . You're a fine, generous woman.

ARKADINA: *(upset)*
I haven't any money!

SORIN:
If I had any myself, it's understandable, I'd give it to
him, but I haven't, not a kopeck. *(laughs)* My
manager takes my whole pension and wastes it on
crops, cattle and bees, and it all goes down the drain.
The bees die, the cows die, and he never lets me have
horses . . .

ARKADINA:
Well, I do have some money. But I'm an actress. My
wardrobe alone is enough to ruin me.

SORIN:
You're a good person, my dear . . . I respect
you . . . Yes . . . But something's coming over me
again. *(sways)* My head's spinning. *(holds
on to the table)* I feel sick or whatever.

ARKADINA: *(frightened)*
  Petrusha!   *(tries to support him)*   Petrusha, my
  darling . . .   *(shouts)*   Help me! Help! . . .

  Enter TREPLYOV, his head bandaged, and
  MEDVEDENKO.

ARKADINA:
  He's sick.

SORIN:
  It's nothing, nothing . . .   *(smiles and drinks some*
  water)   It's already gone . . . or whatever . . .

TREPLYOV: *(to his mother)*
  Don't be frightened, Mama, it's not dangerous. He
  often has these attacks lately. You must lie down for a
  while, Uncle.

SORIN:
  For a little while, yes . . . But I'm still going to town . . .
  I'll lie down for a while, then I'm going . . . it's under-
  standable . . .   *(He goes, leaning on his walking stick.)*

MEDVEDENKO: *(takes his arm)*
  There's a riddle: what goes on four legs in the
  morning, two at noon, three in the evening . . .

SORIN: *(laughs)*
  Precisely. And on its back at night. Thank you, but I
  can manage myself . . .

MEDVEDENKO:
  Come now, no ceremony!   *(He and SORIN exit.)*

ARKADINA:
  How he frightened me!

TREPLYOV:
  It's not healthy for him to live in the country. He gets
  depressed. But if you were suddenly generous, Mama,

56

and could lend him a thousand or two, he could spend a whole year in town.

ARKADINA:
I haven't any money. I'm an actress, not a banker.

Pause.

TREPLYOV:
Mama, change my bandage. You do it so well.

ARKADINA: *(gets some iodine and a box of bandages from the medicine cupboard)*
The doctor's late.

TREPLYOV:
He promised to be here by ten, and it's already noon.

ARKADINA:
Sit down. *(removes his bandage)* You look like you're wearing a turban. Someone dropped by the kitchen yesterday and asked what nationality you were. It's almost healed, though. Nothing much to see. *(kisses him on the head)* And while I'm away, you won't do any more click, click, will you?

TREPLYOV:
No, Mama. It was a moment of mad despair, I couldn't control myself. It won't happen again. *(kisses her hand)* You've such magic hands. I remember a long time ago when you were still acting in the State Theatres.[29] I was just little then. There was a fight in our courtyard, and one of the tenants, a washer-woman, got badly beaten. Remember that? She was picked up unconscious . . . You used to visit her, take her medicine, bathe her children in a tub. Don't you remember?

ARKADINA:
No. *(puts on a fresh bandage)*

57

TREPLYOV:
> There were two ballerinas living in the same house . . .
> They'd come and have coffee with you . . .

ARKADINA:
> That I remember.

TREPLYOV:
> They were very religious. *(pause)* Lately, these
> last few days, I've loved you as tenderly and completely
> as when I was a child. I don't have anyone now except
> you. Only why, why do you let that man influence you?

ARKADINA:
> You don't understand him, Kostya. He's a man of
> fine character . . .

TREPLYOV:
> Yet when he heard I was going to challenge him to a
> duel his fine character didn't stop him playing the
> coward. He's leaving. Running like a dog!

ARKADINA:
> That's ridiculous! I asked him to leave myself.

TREPLYOV:
> Fine character! Here we are almost quarreling over
> him, and right now I'll bet he's somewhere in the
> garden or the drawing-room laughing at us . . .
> enlightening Nina, trying to convince her he's a
> genius.

ARKADINA:
> You enjoy baiting me. I respect that man and I won't
> have you insult him to my face.

TREPLYOV:
> Well, I don't respect him. You want me to think he's
> a genius, too, but I'm sorry, I can't lie. His books
> make me sick.

ARKADINA:

That's just envy. Anyone who's not talented, who's only pretentious, is always running down real talent. I suppose it's comforting!

TREPLYOV: *(sarcastically)*
Real talent! *(angrily)* I'm more talented than the whole pack of you, if it comes to that! *(tears off his bandage)* You, you hacks, you've grabbed control of the arts, you think only what you do has merit! Everything else you stifle and suppress! Well, I don't recognize you! I don't recognize you or him!

ARKADINA:
Decadent! . . .

TREPLYOV:

Go back to your precious theatre and act in your miserable, third-rate plays!

ARKADINA:

I've never acted in third-rate plays. Leave me alone! You're not fit to write bad vaudeville. Kiev shop-keeper! Parasite!

TREPLYOV:
Miser!

ARKADINA:

Beggar! *(TREPLYOV sits down and cries quietly.)* Nobody! *(paces up and down excitedly)* Don't cry. You mustn't cry . . . *(she cries)* Don't . . . *(kisses his forehead, his cheeks, his head)* My darling child, forgive me . . . Forgive your wicked mother. Forgive me, I'm so unhappy.

TREPLYOV: *(embraces her)*
If you only knew! I've lost everything. She doesn't love me, I can't write anymore . . . It's all gone, everything I'd hoped for.

ARKADINA:
Don't despair . . . It'll all work out. He'll be gone
soon, and she'll love you again.   *(wipes away his
tears)*   That's enough. We've made up now.

TREPLYOV: *(kisses her hands)*
Yes, Mama.

ARKADINA: *(tenderly)*
Make up with him, too. There's no need for a
duel . . . Now is there?

TREPLYOV:
All right . . . Only please, Mama, don't make me see
him. It's too much . . . I couldn't bear it . . .
(TRIGORIN enters.)   There . . . I'm going . . .
(quickly puts the dressings in the cupboard)   The doctor
can do my bandage later . . .

TRIGORIN: *(looking through the book)*
Page 121 . . . lines 11 and 12 . . . Here it is . . .
(reads)   "If you should ever need my life, come and
take it."

> *TREPLYOV picks up the bandage from the floor and exits.*

ARKADINA: *(looking at her watch)*
The horses will be here soon.

TRIGORIN: *(to himself)*
"If you should ever need my life, come and take it."

ARKADINA:
You finished packing, I hope?

TRIGORIN: *(impatiently)*
Yes, yes . . .   *(musing)*   Why do I find it so
sad, this cry from an innocent soul? Why does it wring
my heart? . . . "If you should ever need my life, come
and take it."   *(to ARKADINA)*   Let's stay one
more day!

ARKADINA shakes her head.

TRIGORIN:
Let's stay!

ARKADINA:
Darling, I know what's holding you here, but have some control. You're a little intoxicated. Sober up.

TRIGORIN:
You be sober, too. Be intelligent, be sensible. Please. Look at this like a true friend . . .   *(presses her hand)*   You're capable of sacrifice . . . Be my friend, let me go.

ARKADINA: *(greatly upset)*
You're that infatuated?

TRIGORIN:
I'm drawn to her! Maybe it's just what I need.

ARKADINA:
The love of some provincial girl? Oh, how little you know yourself!

TRIGORIN:
Sometimes people walk in their sleep. And that's how I am now. I'm talking to you but it's as if I were asleep, dreaming of her . . . I'm possessed by sweet, wonderful dreams . . . Let me go . . .

ARKADINA: *(trembling)*
No, no . . . I'm just an ordinary woman, you mustn't talk to me like that . . . Don't torture me, Boris . . . I'm terrified . . .

TRIGORIN:
You could be extraordinary, if you wanted to. A love that's young, enchanting, poetic, that carries you off into a world of dreams, it's the only thing on earth can ever give you happiness! I've never known a love

like that . . . There wasn't time when I was young. I was always beating down the doors of editors' offices, fighting to make a living . . . Now here it is, that love. It's come at last, it's beckoning . . . Why should I run from it?

ARKADINA: *(angrily)*
You're out of your mind!

TRIGORIN:
What if I am?

ARKADINA:
You've all conspired today just to torment me. *(weeps)*

TRIGORIN: *(clutches his head)*
She doesn't understand! She doesn't want to understand!

ARKADINA:
Am I really that old and ugly that you think you can talk to me about other women? *(embraces and kisses him)* Oh, you're mad! My beautiful, marvellous . . . You, the last page of my life! *(falls on her knees)* My joy, my pride, my happiness . . . *(embraces his knees)* If you leave me even for an hour, I'll never survive. I'll go mad, my wonderful, magnificent man, my master . . .

TRIGORIN:
Someone might come in. *(helps her up)*

ARKADINA:
Let them, I'm not ashamed of my love for you. *(kisses his hands)* My darling reckless boy, you want to run wild, but I won't have it, I won't let you . . . *(laughs)* You're mine . . . You're mine . . . This brow's mine, and these eyes, and this beautiful silky hair . . . You're all mine. You're so talented, so intelligent, the best writer alive, you're Russia's only hope . . . You've such sincerity, simplicity, freshness,

robust humour . . . In one stroke you get the very
essence of a character or landscape. Your characters
are so alive. Oh, it's impossible to read you without
ecstasy! You think this is hero worship? You think I'm
just flattering you? Come, look into my eyes . . .
Look . . . Are these the eyes of a liar? There, you see,
I'm the only one who appreciates you, the only one
who tells you the truth, my wonderful darling . . . Will
you come with me? Yes? You won't leave me? . . .

TRIGORIN:

I've no will of my own . . . never had. Weak,
spineless, submissive as always. Can a woman really
find that appealing? Take me, take me away, but
don't let me out of your sight, not for a moment . . .

ARKADINA: *(to herself)*
Now he's mine.   *(casually, as if nothing had
happened)*   But, of course, you can stay if you like.
I'll go by myself, and you can come later, in a week.
After all, what's the hurry?

TRIGORIN:
No, we'll go together.

ARKADINA:
Whatever you like. Together then . . .   *(Pause.
TRIGORIN makes a note in his book.)*   What's that?

TRIGORIN:
I heard a good phrase this morning — "virgin pines."
Might come in handy.   *(stretches)*   So we're
going, are we? More railway carriages, stations,
refreshment bars, veal cutlets, conversations . . .

SHAMRAYEV enters.

SHAMRAYEV:
I have the sad honour to announce that the horses are
ready. It's time to leave for the station, dear lady,
the train arrives at five past two. And you will do me

that one small favour, won't you Irina Nikolayevna? You won't forget to make an inquiry: Where is the actor Suzdaltsev now? Is he still alive? Is he well? We used to drink together once . . . He was perfect in *The Mail Robbery*[30] . . . I remember the tragedian Ismaylov, also a remarkable personality . . . he was in the same company with him at Elizavetgrad. There's no hurry, dear lady, you've got another five minutes. They were playing conspirators once in some melodrama, and when they were discovered, he had to say, "We're caught in a trap," but Ismaylov said, "We're traught in a clap." *(laughs loudly)* Clap! . . .

While he talks, YAKOV is busy with the suitcases. The MAID brings ARKADINA her hat, coat, parasol, gloves. All help ARKADINA to put them on. The COOK peers in through the door on the left, hesitates, then enters. POLINA enters followed by MEDVEDENKO.

POLINA: *(with a basket)*
Here are some plums for the journey . . . They're very sweet. In case you feel like a little something . . .

ARKADINA:
You're very kind.

POLINA:
Goodbye, my dear! I'm sorry if everything hasn't been quite right.   *(weeps)*

ARKADINA: *(embracing her)*
Everything's been fine, just fine. Only you mustn't cry.

POLINA:
Our time is passing!

ARKADINA:
There's nothing we can do about that!

SORIN: *(Enters wearing an overcoat with a cape, his hat on, and his walking stick in his hand. He comes in from the door on the left and crosses the stage.)* Sister, it's time, if you don't want to be late, and everything. Really . . . I'll be in the carriage. *(exits)*

MEDVEDENKO:
I'll walk to the station . . . to see you off. I'm a fast walker . . . *(exits)*

ARKADINA:
Goodbye, darlings . . . We'll meet again next summer, if we're alive and well. *(The MAID, YAKOV and the COOK kiss her hand.)* Don't forget me. *(Gives the COOK a ruble)* Here's a ruble for the three of you.

COOK:
Thank you kindly, Ma'am. Have a pleasant journey! We appreciate your kindness!

YAKOV:
Godspeed!

SHAMRAYEV:
A little letter would make us so happy! Goodbye, Boris Alekseyevich!

ARKADINA:
Where's Constantine? Tell him I'm leaving. We must say goodbye, now. Well, think kindly of me. *(to YAKOV)* I gave the cook a ruble. It's for all three of you.

All exit right. The stage is empty. Offstage, the sounds of leave-taking. The MAID returns to get the basket of plums from the table and exits again.

TRIGORIN: *(returning)*
I forgot my walking stick. I think it's on the terrace. *(He goes towards the door on the left and meets NINA coming in.)* It's you! We're leaving.

NINA:

    I knew we'd see each other again. *(excitedly)*
Boris Alekseyevich, I've made up my mind once and
for all. The die is cast, I'm going on the stage. I'll be
gone by tomorrow. I'm leaving my father, giving up
everything, starting a new life . . . I'm leaving, like
you . . . for Moscow. We could see each other there.

TRIGORIN: *(glancing around)*

    Stay at the Slavyansky Bazaar . . . Let me know at
once . . . Molchanovka, Grokholsky House . . . I must
hurry . . . *(pause)*

NINA:

    One more minute . . . .

TRIGORIN: *(in a low voice)*

    You're so lovely . . . to think we shall see each other
soon! *(She rests her head on his chest.)* I'll see
these lovely eyes again, this inexpressibly beautiful,
tender smile . . . these gentle features, this look of
angelic purity . . . My darling . . . *(a prolonged
kiss)*

      Curtain

There is an interval of two years between Act Three and Act Four.

ACT FOUR

*A drawing-room in SORIN's house, which TREPLYOV
has converted into a study. Doors on the right and left
lead into other rooms. In the centre is a French window
that opens onto the terrace. Besides the usual furniture,
there is a writing desk in the right corner, an ottoman
near the door on the left, a bookcase, and books on the
windowsills and chairs.*

*Evening. A single shaded lamp is lit. The room is in
semi-darkness. Sound of trees rustling and wind howling
in the chimneys. The watchman is tapping.[31] Enter
MEDVEDENKO and MASHA.*

MASHA: *(calling)*
Constantine! Constantine! *(looking round)*
There's no one here. Every other minute the old man
asks, "Where's Kostya? Where's Kostya?" He can't
live without him . . . .

MEDVEDENKO:
He's afraid of being alone. *(listening)* What
terrible weather. Two whole days now.

MASHA: *(turning up the lamp)*
There are waves on the lake. Huge waves.

MEDVEDENKO:
It's dark in the garden. We should have had that stage
pulled down. It stands there, bare and ugly like a

67

skeleton, its curtain flapping in the wind. Last night when I passed there, I thought I heard someone crying.

MASHA:
What next . . .   *(pause)*

MEDVEDENKO:
Let's go home, Masha!

MASHA: *(shakes her head)*
I'm staying here tonight.

MEDVEDENKO: *(imploringly)*
Masha, let's go! The baby must be hungry.

MASHA:
Nonsense. Matryona will feed it.   *(pause)*

MEDVEDENKO:
It's hard on him. Three nights without his mother.

MASHA:
You've become a bore. At one time you'd at least philosophize a bit, but now it's all home and baby, home and baby. All I ever hear.

MEDVEDENKO:
Let's go, Masha!

MASHA:
Go yourself.

MEDVEDENKO:
Your father won't give me a horse.

MASHA:
He will if you ask him.

MEDVEDENKO:
All right, I'll try. Will you be home tomorrow?

MASHA: *(takes a pinch of snuff)*
    All right, tomorrow. Stop pestering me . . . .

    Enter TREPLYOV and POLINA. TREPLYOV carries
    pillows and a blanket, POLINA sheets and pillowcases.
    They lay them on the ottoman. TREPLYOV crosses and
    sits down at his desk.

MASHA:
    What's that for, Mama?

POLINA:
    Peter Nikolayevich asked to have his bed made up in
    Kostya's room.

MASHA:
    Let me do it . . .   *(makes the bed)*

POLINA: *(sighing)*
    Old people, they're like children . . . .   *(Goes to the*
    desk, leans on her elbow, and looks at a manuscript. Pause)

MEDVEDENKO:
    Well, I'm going. Goodbye, Masha.   *(kisses his wife's*
    hand)   Goodbye, Mama.   *(tries to kiss his mother-*
    in-law's hand)

POLINA: *(annoyed)*
    Well, go if you're going.

MEDVEDENKO:
    Goodbye, Constantine Gavrilych.

    TREPLYOV silently shakes hands. MEDVEDENKO
    exits.

POLINA: *(looking at the manuscript)*
    No one ever thought you'd become a real writer,
    Kostya. But now, thank goodness, the magazines are
    even starting to pay you.   *(strokes his hair)*   And

you've grown so handsome, too . . . Dear, good
Kostya, be kinder to my Mashenka . . .

MASHA: *(making the bed)*
Let him alone, Mama.

POLINA: *(to TREPLYOV)*
She's such a nice girl.   *(pause)*   A woman
doesn't need much, Kostya, just a kind look. Believe
me, I know.

> *TREPLYOV gets up from his desk and leaves without a
> word.*

MASHA:
Now he's angry. Why must you pester him?

POLINA:
I feel sorry for you, Mashenka.

MASHA:
A lot of good that does.

POLINA:
My heart aches for you. I see it all, you know. I
understand.

MASHA:
It's all foolishness. That's only in novels, unrequited
love. It's rubbish. The thing is not to give in to it, not
to be always waiting for something, waiting for the
tide to turn . . . If love steals into your heart, stamp it
out. They've promised to transfer my husband to
another district. Once we get there, I'll forget all
this . . . I'll tear it out of my heart by the roots.

> *Two rooms away a melancholy waltz is played.*

POLINA:
That's Kostya. He must be depressed.

MASHA: *(waltzes a few steps in silence)*
The main thing, Mama, is not to see him. Believe me,
if they'd only give my Semyon a transfer, I'd forget all
this in a month. It's such rubbish.

> *The door on the left opens. DORN and
> MEDVEDENKO enter, wheeling SORIN in his
> wheelchair.*

MEDVEDENKO:
There are six of us at home now. And flour costs two
kopecks a pound.

DORN:
It's a tight squeeze.

MEDVEDENKO:
It's fine for you to laugh. You're rolling in money.

DORN:
Money? In thirty years of practice, my friend, when I
could barely call my soul my own, I managed to
scrape together a mere two thousand rubles. And I just
spent that on a trip abroad. I haven't a kopeck.

MASHA: *(to her husband)*
Haven't you left yet?

MEDVEDENKO: *(guiltily)*
How can I, when they won't give me a horse!

MASHA: *(bitterly annoyed, in a low voice)*
I wish I'd never set eyes on you!

> *The wheelchair stops stage left. POLINA, MASHA and
> DORN sit down close by. MEDVEDENKO, hangdog,
> stands apart.*

DORN:
So many changes though! I see you've turned the
drawing-room into a study.

71

MASHA:
Constantine Gavrilych finds it handier to work here.
When he wants to he can go out in the garden and
think.

> *The watchman taps.*

SORIN:
Where's my sister?

DORN:
She went to the station to meet Trigorin. She'll be
back any minute.

SORIN:
If you felt you had to send for my sister, I must be
seriously ill.   *(after a pause)*   Strange, isn't it?
I'm seriously ill, but they don't give me any medicine.

DORN:
What would you like? Valerian drops? Soda? Quinine?

SORIN:
Oh, here it comes, the lecture. That's suffering
enough!   *(nods towards the ottoman)*   Is that for
me?

POLINA:
For you, Peter Nikolayevich.

SORIN:
Thank you.

DORN: *(sings softly)*
"The moon floats by in the evening sky . . ."

SORIN:
I'd like to give Kostya an idea for a story. It should be
called, *"The Man Who Wanted — L'homme qui a voulu."*
When I was young, I wanted to be a writer . . . and
didn't. I wanted to speak well . . . and spoke

abominably. *(mimics himself)* "And so on and so forth, what have you, and all the rest of it . . . if you know what I mean." When I was summing up, I'd drag on and on till I broke into a sweat. I wanted to get married . . . and didn't. I always wanted to live in town . . . and here I am ending my days in the country, and . . . so on . . .

DORN:
You wanted to become a State Councillor — and you did.

SORIN: *(laughing)*
I never aimed for that. It just happened.

DORN:
To be blaming life at sixty-two is hardly magnanimous.

SORIN:
You're so pigheaded. Can't you understand? I want to live.

DORN:
That's fatuous. According to the laws of nature every life must have an end.

SORIN:
Spoken like a man who's had his fill. You're satisfied, so you don't care if you live or not, to you it's all the same. But death will be terrifying, even for you.

DORN:
The fear of death's an animal fear . . . One must overcome it. It's reasonable to fear death if you believe in eternal life and you're frightened for your sins. But in the first place, you're not a believer, and in the second, what sins have you committed? You've worked in the Department of Justice for twenty-five years, that's all.

SORIN: *(laughing)*
   Twenty-eight . . .

> *TREPLYOV enters and sits on a stool at SORIN's feet.*
> *MASHA never takes her eyes off him.*

DORN:
   We're keeping Constantine Gavrilovich from his work.

TREPLYOV:
   It doesn't matter.   *(pause)*

MEDVEDENKO:
   If I may ask, Doctor, which town abroad did you like
   the best?

DORN:
   Genoa.

TREPLYOV:
   Why Genoa?

DORN:
   The street life there is marvellous. In the evening
   when you leave your hotel, the whole street is surging
   with people. You drift with the crowd, aimlessly,
   moving in all directions. You become part of its life,
   you merge with it psychically, until finally you begin
   to believe there might really be a World Soul after all,
   like the one Nina Zarechnaya acted in your play. By
   the way, where is Nina now? And how is she?

TREPLYOV:
   She's well, I suppose.

DORN:
   They say she's been leading a strange sort of life.
   What happened?

TREPLYOV:
   That, Doctor, is a long story.

DORN:

    Make is short then.   *(pause)*

TREPLYOV:

    She ran away and had an affair with Trigorin. You
knew that?

DORN:

    Yes.

TREPLYOV:

    She had a child. It died. Trigorin got tired of her and
resumed his former attachments, as might be expected.
He never really gave them up anyway. True to his
spineless nature he managed to keep them both going.
As far as I can tell, Nina's personal life was a complete
failure.

DORN:

    And what about her career?

TREPLYOV:

    Even worse, I think. She started in a summer theatre
near Moscow, then went to the provinces. At the time
I never let her out of my sight. I followed wherever
she went. She always got big parts, but her acting was
crude and tasteless, she ranted and hammed it up. She
had good moments, when she was screaming or dying,
but they were only moments.

DORN;

    Then she does have talent?

TREPLYOV:

    It's hard to say. I think so. I saw her, but she refused
to see me, and her maid wouldn't let me in the hotel
room. I understand how she felt so I didn't insist.
(pause)   What more can I tell you? Later, when I
came back home, she wrote me a few times. Her
letters were intelligent, warm, interesting. She never
complained, but I could sense she was deeply unhappy

Every line she wrote showed nervous exhaustion. She'd also got this strange idea in her head. She always signed herself "The Seagull." Just as the miller in Pushkin's *River Nymph*[32] calls himself a raven, she called herself a seagull in all her letters. Now she's here.

DORN:
What do you mean, here?

TREPLYOV:
It town, staying at an inn. She's been here five days now. I would've gone to see her, but Masha drove in, and she won't see anyone. Semyon claims he saw her in the fields yesterday after dinner, a mile or so from here.

MEDVEDENKO:
That's right, I did. She was walking away from here, towards town. I bowed and asked why she hadn't been out to see us. She said she'd come.

TREPLYOV:
She won't. *(pause)* Her father and stepmother won't have anything to do with her. They've posted watchmen to keep her off the grounds. *(crosses to the desk with DORN)* How easy it is, Doctor, to be a philosopher on paper, and how hard it is in life!

SORIN:
She was a delightful girl.

DORN:
What was that?

SORIN:
I said she was a delightful girl. State Councillor Sorin was even in love with her himself for a while.

DORN:
You old Lovelace.

SHAMRAYEV's laugh is heard offstage.

POLINA:
  I think they're back from the station . . .

TREPLYOV:
  Yes, that sounds like Mama.

  *Enter ARKADINA and TRIGORIN, followed by
  SHAMRAYEV.*

SHAMRAYEV: *(coming in)*
  We all get old and weather-beaten, dear lady, but you,
  you're still young . . . A light dress, vivacity . . .
  grace . . .

ARKADINA:
  You want to bring me bad luck again, you boring
  man!

TRIGORIN: *(to SORIN)*
  Peter Nikolayevich, what're you doing still sick? That's
  no good! *(delighted to see MASHA)* Masha!

MASHA:
  You recognize me? *(shakes his hand)*

TRIGORIN:
  Married?

MASHA:
  Long ago.

TRIGORIN:
  Happy? *(bows to DORN and MEDVEDENKO, who
  bow in return, then hesitantly approaches TREPLYOV)*
  Irina Nikolayevna tells me you've forgotten the past.
  You're not angry anymore. *(TREPLYOV holds out
  his hand.)*

ARKADINA: *(to her son)*
Look, Boris has the magazine with your new story.

TREPLYOV: *(Takes the magazine. To TRIGORIN)*
Thank you. You're very kind. *(They sit down.)*

TRIGORIN:
Your admirers send their respects . . . There's a lot of
interest in your work in Petersburg and Moscow, and
I'm always being asked about you: What's he like?
How old is he? Is he dark or fair? For some reason
they all think you can't be young. And no one knows
your real name because you write under a pseudonym.
You're a mystery, like the Man in the Iron Mask.

TREPLYOV:
Will you be staying long?

TRIGORIN:
No, I think I'll leave for Moscow tomorrow. I must.
I'm in a hurry to finish my story, and besides, I
promised to write something for an anthology. In other
words, it's the same old thing.

> *While they are talking, ARKADINA and POLINA set
> a card table in the middle of the room and open it up.
> SHAMRAYEV lights candles and sets up the chairs. A
> game of lotto[33] is brought out of the cupboard.*

TRIGORIN:
The weather's given me a poor welcome. There's a
fierce wind. If it slacks off by morning, I'll go fishing
on the lake. I must have a look round the garden and
the place where . . . do you remember? . . . your play
was done. I've an idea in mind for a short story, but I
want to refresh my memory of the setting.

MASHA: *(to her father)*
Papa, let Semyon have a horse! He has to get home.

SHAMRAYEV: *(mimics her)*
A horse . . . Has to get home . . .   *(sternly)*   See
for yourself: they're just back from the station. They're
not going out again.

MASHA:
But there are other horses . . .   *(When her father says
nothing, she makes a gesture of exasperation.)*   Oh,
you're impossible . . .

MEDVEDENKO:
I can walk, Masha. Really . . .

POLINA: *(sighs)*
Walk, in this weather . . .   *(sits down at the card
table)*   Come on, friends.

MEDVEDENKO:
After all, it's only four miles . . . Goodbye . . .   *(kisses
his wife's hand)*   Goodbye, Mama.   *(His mother-
in-law reluctantly puts out her hand for him to kiss.)*   I
wouldn't have bothered anyone; it's the baby . . .
(bows to everyone)   Goodbye . . .   *(exits apologetically)*

SHAMRAYEV:
He'll make it on foot. He's no general.

POLINA: *(taps on the table)*
Come along, friends. Let's not waste time, they'll be
calling us for supper soon.

> *SHAMRAYEV, MASHA and DORN sit down at the
> table.*

ARKADINA: *(to TRIGORIN)*
They always play lotto here in the long autumn
evenings. Look, the old lotto set we had when my
mother played with us children. Wouldn't you like a
game before supper?   *(She sits at the table with
TRIGORIN.)*   It's a boring game, but it's not bad

79

once you get used to it.   *(deals everyone three cards)*

TREPLYOV: *(turning the pages of the magazine)*
He's read his own story, but he hasn't even cut the pages of mine.   *(Puts the magazine on the desk, then starts for the door on the left. As he passes his mother, he kisses her on the head.)*

ARKADINA:
What about you, Kostya?

TREPLYOV:
Sorry, but I don't feel like it . . . I'm going for a walk.   *(exits)*

ARKADINA:
The stakes are ten kopecks. Put it in for me, will you, Doctor.

DORN:
At your service.

MASHA:
Are all the stakes in? I'll start . . . Twenty-two!

ARKADINA:
I have it.

MASHA:
Three!

DORN:
There we are.

MASHA:
Did you put down three? Eight! Eighty-one! Ten!

SHAMRAYEV:
Not so fast.

ARKADINA:
How they loved me at Kharkoff. Goodness, my head's still spinning!

MASHA:
Thirty-four!

A sad waltz is heard offstage.

ARKADINA:
The students gave me a standing ovation . . . three baskets of flowers, two garlands, and this . . . *(removes a brooch and throws it on the table)*

SHAMRAYEV:
Yes, that's the real . . .

MASHA:
Fifty!

DORN:
Fifty, even?

ARKADINA:
My costume was stunning . . . Say what you like, I do know how to dress.

POLINA:
Kostya's at the piano. He's depressed, poor boy.

SHAMRAYEV:
They've been attacking him in the newspapers.

MASHA:
Seventy-seven!

ARKADINA:
Who cares what they say?

TRIGORIN:
He hasn't much luck. Hasn't found his own voice yet.

Something strange about it, vague, even disturbed. His characters don't live.

MASHA:
  Eleven!

ARKADINA: *(looking round at SORIN)*
  Petrusha, are you bored? *(pause)* He's asleep.

DORN:
  State Councillor Sorin is asleep.

MASHA:
  Seven! Ninety!

TRIGORIN:
  If I lived on this estate beside this lake, do you think I'd write? I'd conquer the passion and do nothing but fish.

MASHA:
  Twenty-eight!

TRIGORIN:
  To catch a perch or a chub — what bliss!

DORN:
  Well, I believe in Constantine Gavrilovich. There's something there! Something there! He thinks in images. His stories are intense, colourful, moving. It's just a pity he has no definite aim. He makes an impression, nothing more, and that's not enough. Irina Nikolayevna, are you glad your son's a writer?

ARKADINA:
  Believe it or not, I've never read him. Can't find the time.

MASHA:
  Twenty-six!

TREPLYOV enters without speaking and goes to his desk.

SHAMRAYEV: *(to TRIGORIN)*
By the way, Boris Alekseyevich, we've still got something belongs to you.

TRIGORIN:
What's that?

SHAMRAYEV:
Constantine Gavrilych shot a seagull once, and you asked me to have it stuffed.

TRIGORIN:
I don't remember. *(thinking)* I don't remember!

MASHA:
Sixty-six! One!

TREPLYOV: *(throws open the window and listens)*
It's so dark out! I don't know why I feel so uneasy.

ARKADINA:
Kostya, shut the window, there's a draught. *(TREPLYOV shuts the window.)*

MASHA:
Eighty-eight!

TRIGORIN:
My game, ladies and gentlemen.

ARKADINA: *(gaily)*
Bravo! Bravo!

SHAMRAYEV:
Bravo!

ARKADINA:
He's lucky in everything, this man.   *(rises)*   And now let's go have a bite to eat. Our famous writer missed lunch today. We'll continue after supper. *(to her son)*   Leave your writing. Kostya, and come and eat.

TREPLYOV:
I don't want to, Mama. I'm not hungry.

ARKADINA:
Whatever you like.   *(wakes SORIN)*   Petrusha, supper!   *(takes SHAMRAYEV's arm)*   I'll tell you about my reception in Kharkoff . . .

> *POLINA puts out the candles on the table. Then she and DORN wheel out the wheelchair. All exit by the door, left. TREPLYOV remains alone on stage, sitting at his desk.*

TREPLYOV: *(Ready to write, he reads through what he has already written.)*
I've talked so much about new forms, but now I feel myself slipping into a rut, little by little.   *(reads)* "The placards on the wall announced" . . . "A pale face, framed with dark hair" . . . "Announced . . . framed . . ." That's flat.[34]   *(crosses it out)*   I'll start where the hero's awakened by the rain, and the rest goes. The description of the moonlit evening's long and forced. Trigorin's worked out his own method, it's easy for him . . . He describes the neck of a broken bottle glittering on a dam and the black shadow of a mill wheel — and there's your moonlit night.[35] But with me it's the shimmering light, the silent twinkling of the stars, the distant sounds of a piano dying on the still, fragrant air . . . It's excruciating. *(pause)*   Yes, more and more I've come to see it's not a matter of old or new forms. A man should write without thinking of form at all. He should write straight from the heart.   *(a knock on the window nearest the desk)*   What was that?   *(looks out the*

window) Can't see a thing . . . *(opens the French window and looks into the garden)* Someone ran down the steps. *(calls)* Who's there? *(He exits. He can be heard walking quickly along the terrace. Half a minute later he returns with NINA.)* Nina! Nina!

NINA rests her head on his chest and sobs quietly.

TREPLYOV: *(moved)*
Nina! Nina! It's you . . . you . . . I had a feeling, all day my heart's been aching. *(removes her hat and cloak)* My angel, light of my eyes, she's come. Let's not cry, let's not.

NINA:
There's someone here.

TREPLYOV:
There's no one.

NINA:
Lock the doors. Someone might come in.

TREPLYOV:
No one'll come in.

NINA:
I know Irina Nikolayevna's here. Lock the doors . . .

TREPLYOV: *(locks the door on the right, then crosses to the door on the left)*
This one doesn't lock. I'll put a chair against it. *(puts an armchair against the door)* Don't be afraid, no one'll come in.

NINA: *(searching his face intently)*
Let me look at you. *(looks around the room)* It's nice here, warm . . . This used to be the drawing-room. Have I changed much?

TREPLYOV:

Yes . . . You're thinner, and your eyes are bigger.
Nina, it's so strange to see you. Why wouldn't you
meet me? Why didn't you come before? I know you've
been here almost a week . . . I've been to the inn
several times a day, I stood under your window like a
beggar.

NINA:

I was afraid you hated me. Every night I dream you
look at me and don't recognize me. If you only knew.
From the moment I arrived, I've been walking around
here . . . by the lake. I've been near the house many
times, but I couldn't bring myself to come in. Let's sit
down.   *(They sit.)*   Let's sit and talk and talk.
It's so nice here, so warm and cozy . . . Hear the
wind? There's a passage in Turgenev: "Happy is he
who has a roof over his head on a night like this, a
warm corner of his own." I'm the seagull . . . No,
that's not right.   *(rubs her forehead)*   What was I
saying? Oh, yes . . . Turgenev . . . "And may the
Lord help all homeless wanderers."[36] It's nothing.
(weeps bitterly)

TREPLYOV:

Nina, you're crying again . . . Nina!

NINA:

It's nothing. It makes me feel better . . . I haven't
cried in two years. I went to the garden late last night
to see if our stage was still there. It's still standing. I
cried for the first time in two years, and I felt lighter,
my soul was clearer. See, I'm not crying anymore.
(takes his hand)   So you're a writer now . . . You're
a writer and I'm an actress . . . We've both fallen into
the whirlpool . . . I lived happily, like a child — you'd
wake up in the morning, singing. I loved you, dreamed
of fame. And now? Early tomorrow I must go to
Yelets . . . third class . . . with the peasants, and at
Yelets the cultured merchants will pester me with their
advances. Life is sordid.

TREPLYOV:
Why Yelets?

NINA:
I've got an engagement there for the winter. It's time
I left.

TREPLYOV:
Nina, I cursed you, hated you, I tore up your letters
and photographs, yet every moment I knew my soul
was bound to you forever. I can't stop loving you,
Nina. I'm not strong enough. Since I lost you and
began getting published, my life's been unbearable . . .
I'm suffering . . . All of a sudden my youth was torn
away and I feel ninety years old. I call your name. I
kiss the ground you walked on; wherever I look I see
your face, the tender smile that shone for me in the
best years of my life . . .

NINA: *(bewildered)*
Why does he talk like this? Why does he talk like this?

TREPLYOV:
I'm alone, I lack the warmth of affection. I'm cold,
cold as in a dungeon, and whatever I write, it's dry,
harsh, gloomy. Stay here, Nina, *please*, or let me go
with you! *(NINA quickly puts on her hat and cloak.)*
Nina, why? For God's sake, Nina! . . . *(Watches as
she puts on her things. Pause.)*

NINA:
My horses are at the gate. Don't see me out, I'll
manage myself . . . *(close to tears)* Give me
some water . . .

TREPLYOV: *(gives her water)*
Where are you going now?

NINA:
To town. *(pause)* Is Irina Nikolayevna here?

87

TREPLYOV:

Yes . . . Uncle took ill on Thursday, so we wired her to come.

NINA:

Why do you say you kiss the ground I walked on? I ought to be killed. *(leans on the table)* I'm so tired. If only I could rest . . . rest. *(raises her head)* I'm the seagull . . . That's not right. I'm an actress. Well, it's not important. *(Hears ARKADINA and TRIGORIN laughing. She listens, then runs to the door, left, and looks through the keyhole.)* He's here, too . . . *(returning to TREPLYOV)* Well, it's not important . . . it's nothing . . . Yes . . . He didn't believe in the theatre. He laughed at all my dreams, and gradually I stopped believing myself and lost heart . . . And then there was the anxiety of love, the jealousy, the constant fear for the baby . . . I became petty and common, I put no thought into my acting . . . I didn't know what to do with my hands, how to stand on stage, or how to control my voice. You can't imagine what it's like to know you're acting badly. I'm the seagull. No, that's not right . . . Remember, you shot a seagull? A man happens along, see her and out of nothing better to do, destroys her . . . An idea for a short story. That's not right . . . *(rubs her forehead)* What was I. . . ? Oh, yes, the theatre. I'm not like that now . . . I'm a real actress. I enjoy acting, I revel in it. I'm drunk when I'm on the stage, and I feel that I'm beautiful. All the time I've been here, I've done nothing but walk. I walk and I think. I think, and I feel my spirit getting stronger by the day . . . Now I know, Kostya, I understand that in our work as actors or writers what's important isn't fame or glory or the things I used to dream about. What's important is knowing how to endure, how to bear your cross and have faith. I have faith and things don't hurt me so much, and when I think of my calling I'm no longer afraid of life.

TREPLYOV: (*sadly*)
> You've found your road, you know where you're
> going, but I'm still drifting in a chaos of dreams and
> images not knowing why I write or who it's for. I've
> no faith and I don't know what my calling is.

NINA: (*listening*)
> Ssh . . . I'm going now. Goodbye. When I'm a great
> actress, come and watch me. Promise? But now . . .
> (*presses his hand*)   It's late. I can hardly
> stand . . . I'm exhausted, I want to eat . . .

TREPLYOV:
> Stay, I'll get you some supper . . .

NINA:
> No, no . . . Don't see me out, I can manage . . . My
> horses are nearby . . . So she brought him with her?
> Well, it doesn't matter. When you see Trigorin don't
> say anything . . . I love him. I love him even more
> than before . . . An idea for a short story . . . I love
> him passionately, desperately. It used to be so nice,
> Kostya. Remember? Our life was so bright and warm,
> so happy, so innocent, and the things we felt as tender
> and delicate as flowers . . . Remember?   (*recites*)
> "Men, lions, eagles and partridges, antlered deer,
> geese, spiders, the silent fish of the deep, starfish and
> creatures invisible to the eye — these and all life have
> run their melancholy cycle and are no more. Thousands
> of centuries have passed since there was life on earth.
> In vain now does the pale moon light her lamp. The
> cranes no longer awake and cry in the meadows, and
> the May beetles are silent in the lime groves."   (*impulsively embraces TREPLYOV and runs out through the French window*)

TREPLYOV: (*after a pause*)
> It'd be too bad if someone saw her in the garden and
> told Mama. That might upset Mama . . .   (*He
> spends two minutes tearing up all his manuscripts and*

throwing them under the desk. Then he unlocks the door on the right and exits.)

DORN: *(trying to open the door on the left)*
That's strange. The door seems to be locked . . .
(enters and puts the armchair back in its place)   Quite an obstacle course.

> *Enter ARKADINA and POLINA, then YAKOV with bottles, and MASHA, then SHAMRAYEV and TRIGORIN.*

ARKADINA:
Put the claret on the table. And the beer for Boris Alekseyevich. We'll drink as we play. Let's sit down, everyone.

POLINA: *(to YAKOV)*
Bring the tea now, as well.   *(lights the candles and sits at the card table)*

SHAMRAYEV: *(takes TRIGORIN to the cupboard)*
Here's that thing I was telling you about . . .
(takes the stuffed seagull from the cupboard)   Just as you ordered.

TRIGORIN: *(looking at the seagull)*
I don't remember!   *(thinks)*   I don't remember!

> *A shot is heard from offstage, right. Everyone gives a start.*

ARKADINA: *(frightened)*
What was that?

DORN:
Nothing. Something must've exploded in my medicine bag. Don't be alarmed.   *(He goes out through the door on the right and comes back half a minute later.)*   That's what it was. A bottle of ether exploded.   *(sings)*
"Once more before, thee, I stand enchanted . . ."

ARKADINA: *(sitting down at the table)*
Whew, it frightened me. It reminded me of when . . .
(covers her face with her hands)   Everything went
black . . .

DORN: *(leafing through a magazine, to TRIGORIN)*
There was an article in this magazine about two
months ago . . . a letter from America . . . I meant to
ask you about it . . .   *(takes TRIGORIN by the waist
and leads him to the front of the stage)*   since I'm quite
interested in this question . . .   *(lowers his voice)*
Get Irina Nikolayevna out of here. The thing is,
Constantine Gavrilovich just shot himself.

Curtain

Biographical Notes

David French, one of Canada's best known playwrights, is the award-winning author of *Leaving Home, Of the Fields, Lately, One Crack Out, The Riddle of the World, Jitters, Salt-Water Moon, 1949* and a new version of Alexandra Ostrovsky's *The Forest*. His latest work is *Silver Dagger*.

• • •

Dr. Donna Orwin, a specialist in nineteenth century Russian literature, is a Research Associate at the Centre for Russian and East European Studies at the University of Toronto. She is the author of *Tolstoy's Art and Thought, 1847-1880* (Princeton University Press, 1993).

This translation of *The Seagull* is based on the Russian text of the play contained in volume nine of the 1963-64 twelve-volume Soviet edition of Chekhov's works and letters. There were four different recensions of the play. The last one, published first in Chekhov's collected works issued in 1901, with a second edition in 1902, furnished the text for the Soviet edition.

Most of the letters quoted in these notes are from the Heim-Karlinsky *Letters of Anton Chekhov* (reprinted by permission of the publisher). Letters not included in this edition and all other material are in my own translation unless otherwise noted.

I would like to thank Professor Ralph Lindheim for his help in preparing these notes.

Donna Orwin

Here are the stress marks for the Russian words in the text:

Irína Nikoláyevna Arkádina, married name Treplyóva
Cónstantine Gavrílovich Treplyóv (also Gavrílych), also
called Kóstya
Peter Nikoláyevich Sórin
Nína Mikháylovna Zaréchnaya
Ilya Shamráyev
Polína
Másha
Borís Alekséyevich Trigórin
Yevgény Sergéyevich (also Sergéich) Dorn
Semyón Medvedénko
Yákov
Pável Semyónovich Chádin
Grokhólsky
Izmáylov
Khárkov
Kíev
Matryóna
Molchanóvka
Nekrásov
Odéssa
Poltáva
Popríshchin
Púshkin
Rasplyúyev
Sadóvsky
Slavyánsky Bazáar
Suzdáltsev
Tolstóy
Turgénev
Yeléts

The Seagull was first staged at the Aleksandrinsky Theatre in Petersburg on October 17, 1896. It was one of the most celebrated flops in the history of the theatre. With Chekhov's permission, the comic actress Leykeyeva had chosen the night for her benefit performance. Her fans packed the theatre to see *The Seagull*, a new comedy by Anton Chekhov. Puzzled by the quiet beginning of the play, they finally burst into laughter and jeers when Nina (played by the great Komissarzhevskaya, then an unknown) began the play-within-a-play. Chekhov fled the hall at the end of the second act and hid in Levkeyeva's dressing room until it was over. He sneaked out of the theatre and left Petersburg the next day without seeing anyone. The play's failure was probably the most severe trauma of his life.

On subsequent nights at the Aleksandrinsky, before a different kind of audience, the play fared better, but the damage had been done. The theatre administration closed it after five performances because of bad reviews. Two years later, on December 17, 1898, The Moscow Art Theatre revived the play to tremendous acclaim.

• • •

As a realist, Chekhov drew his material from life (see note 27), but he despised *romans à clef* (see note 7). He believed that the artist must imaginatively rework what he observes in order to reveal the truth in it. Everything nonessential must be discarded. Thus Chekhov, unlike Stanislavsky, distinguished between realistic theatre and reality. It is of great psychological interest, therefore, that *The Seagull* contains discernible traces of a specific incident from Chekhov's life.

Lidiya (Lika) Mizinova, a friend of Mariya Chekhova, was desperately in love with Chekhov for a number of years. Chekhov was fond of her, but he could not return her passion. Eventually he succeeded in palming her off on the writer I. N. Potapenko, a close friend. Potapenko, married and with two children, pursued Lika ardently. He finally seduced her in Paris, in the summer of 1894. By fall she was pregnant and alone in Switzerland, where her baby was born. Potapenko abandoned her and moved his family to Petersburg. Lika's little girl died shortly after her return to Russia.

Both Lika and Potapenko recognized their story in the first

version of *The Seagull*, which Chekhov may have revised on their account. He had, in any case, transformed the story to the point where he could deny that his play was based on it.

Selected Further Reading

Chekhov, Anton. *Letters of Anton Chekhov*. Selection, commentary and introduction by Simon Karlinsky, translated by Michael Henry Heim, in collaboration with Simon Karlinsky. New York: Harper & Row, 1973. The commentary is as useful as the letters in this excellent edition.

The Oxford Chekhov. Vol. 2. Translated and edited by Ronald Hingley. London: Oxford University Press, 1967. This volume, which contains Hingley's translation of *The Seagull* and two other plays, is especially valuable for its appendices. Hingley outlines the history of the writing of *The Seagull*. Where recensions differ significantly from one another he quotes the relevant passages, and he also includes remarks pertaining to the play from Chekhov's notebook.

The Sea Gull. Translated by Jean-Claude Van Itallie, commentaries by William M. Hoffman and Daniel Seltzer, notes by Paul Schmidt. New York: Harper & Row, Perennial Library, 1977. The notes to this edition of the play are very helpful on the subject of the theatre.

Jackson, Robert Louis, ed. *Chekhov: A Collection of Critical Essays*. Englewood Cliffs, N.J.: Prentice-Hall, 1967. A good cross section of Chekhov criticism.

Melchinger, Siegfried. *Anton Chekhov*. Translated by Edith Tarcov. New York: Frederick Ungar Publishing, 1972. This book contains an excellent analysis of Chekhov's plays and a history of their production in Europe and America.

Mirsky, D.S. *A History of Russian Literature*. New York: Random House, Vintage Books Edition, 1958. This is perhaps the best book available on the subject in any language.

Valency, Maurice. *The Breaking String: The Plays of Anton Chekhov*. New York: Oxford University Press, 1966. This analysis of Chekhov's plays begins with a history of the Russian theatre.

Notes

1. Many memoirists associate the setting of *The Seagull* with Chekhov's estate Melikhovo, some sixty miles south of Moscow. Chekhov wrote the play there, in 1895. Since Melikhovo is located on a small pond, others believe that Chekhov found his magic lake in the lake district near the northern Russian city of Novgorod. He visited a large estsate there in July 1895 in order to nurse his good friend I. I. Levitan (1861-1900) back to health. The moody painter had tried to shoot himself while staying with a wealthy lady friend. Hingley thinks that Chekhov found seagulls there — there were none near Melikhovo — and substituted one for the woodcock that Levitan had wounded (see note 25). In fact, *chayka* is the Russian word for *gull*; a seagull is *morskaya chayka*. The Russian title of the play, *Chayka*, is translated "The Seagull" in English because the distinction between a gull and a seagull is rarely made.

   The paintings of Levitan and Turgenev's nature descriptions in his *Sportsman's Sketches* will give the foreign reader some idea of Russian landscape and climate.

2. In a letter from Melikhovo (to Suvorin, March 11, 1892), Chekhov uses Medvedenko's catchword himself: ". . . clover seed costs a hundred rubles, and I need more than a hundred rubles' worth of oats for sowing. It's a tight squeeze" *(Vot tut i vertis')*.

3. Medvedenko used the word "indifferentism" *(indifferentizm)* instead of a perfectly good Russian word for indifference *(ravnodushie)*. It sounds as awkward in Russian as it does in English.

4. N. A. Nekrasov (1821-78) was one of the greatest poets of Arkadina's generation, and the hero of the radicals for his call to subordinate art to civic duty. Arkadina would have recited his passionate dramatic verse very well. Nekrasov fell out of favor during the Symbolist revival of poetry.

Chekhov admired him however, and forgave him his faults (his lapses in poetic form) for the power and beauty of his verse.

5. Chekhov saw Eleonora Duse (1859-1924) in Petersburg in 1891, and he described his impressions of her in a letter to his sister:

> I've just seen Duse, the Italian actress, in Shakespeare's *Cleopatra*. I don't understand Italian, but she played so beautifully that I had a feeling that I understood every word. A remarkable actress. I've never seen anything like it. Watching Duse, I was overcome by depression from the thought that we have to form our reactions and taste on such wooden actresses as Yermolova and those like her whom we call great only because we've never seen better. Looking at Duse, I realized why the Russian theatre is such a bore. (March 16, 1891)

6. *Camille*, as it is called in English (*La Dame aux camélias* in the original French) is the famous play by Dumas fils (1824-95) based on his novel of the same name. It was first staged in 1852.

7. *The Fumes of Life* was a melodrama by Boleslav Markevich (1822-1884) based on his *roman à clef, The Abyss*. Chekhov saw this play in 1884 and wrote it up for the column "Fragments of Moscow Life" in the Moscow journal *Fragments (Oskolki)*. "In his works B. Markevich depicts only his close acquaintances — the mark of a writer who can see no farther than the end of his own nose . . . In general this drama is written with a mop and smells to high heavens."

8. V. E. Meyerhold (1874-1940), the great modernist director, played Treplyov in the first Art Theatre production of *The Seagull*. For him these lines summed up everything hateful about realist drama. In 1921 he flung them at the Art Theatre itself. It was "a whole army of actors, psychologically 'experiencing' the parts of all those characters who do nothing but walk, eat, drink, make love and wear jackets" (from "The Solitude of Stanislavsky" in *Vestnik teatra*, 1921, nos. 87-88; reprinted in *Meyerhold on Theatre*, ed. Edward Braun [Chatham, 1969]).

Chekhov also wanted to reform conventional theatre, but

he insisted on a realism of which Treplyov and Meyerhold would disapprove. In 1889 in Yalta he explained what he expected of the theatre to I. Ya. Gurlyand:

> Really, in life people are not every minute shooting each other, hanging themselves, and making declarations of love. And they are not saying clever things every minute. For the most part, they eat, drink, hang about, and talk nonsense; and this must be seen on the stage. A play must be written in which people can come, do, dine, talk about the weather, and play cards, not because that's the way the author wants it, but because that's the way it happens in real life.
>
> Let everything on the stage be just as complex and at the same time as simple as in life. People dine, merely dine, but at that moment their happiness is being made or their life is being smashed.
>
> (Skaftymov, "Principles of Structure in Chekhov's Plays" in Jackson, p. 73, reprinted by permission of the publisher)

9. This word, *meshchanin*, is a stumbling block for all translators of *The Seagull*. It refers to free town-dwellers, originally a hereditary class, who in Russia never attained the importance of the bourgeoisie in Western Europe. The *meshchane* were despised by the landed gentry, from whose ranks Arkadina comes. By the end of the nineteenth century this word had acquired all the associations of "petty bourgeois." Thus Gorky's first play, entitled *Meshchane* (1901), is variously translated into English as *The Philistines, The Petty Bourgeois,* or *The Smug Citizens*.

10. "Two Grenadiers" (*Die beiden Grenadiere*, 1840) is a poem by Heinrich Heine (1797-1856) set to music by Robert Schumann (1810-56). It was translated into Russian by M. L. Mikhaylov (1829-65).

11. Chekhov thinks that art should depict "life as it is and should be." See his November 25, 1892 letter to Suvorin in note 27. (Alexey Suvorin [1834-1912], to whom Chekhov wrote most of his important letters, was one of the first publishers to recognize Chekhov's talents. He published most of Chekhov's first serious stories in his newspaper *New Times* in 1886-87.)

12. "Say not that youth has perished" is a popular song based on a poem by Nekrasov ("A heavy cross she had to bear in sorrow").

13. "Once more before thee" is a popular song based on a poem entitled "Stanzas" by V. I. Krasov (1810-55).

14. When the famous Russian actor V. I. Kachhalov was rehearsing Trigorin, Chekhov invited him to discuss the role, and Kachalov recalled this conversation in his memoirs. (Apparently Chekhov felt shy about giving advice in person, and Kachalov tries to convey this in his speech.)

> "You know," began Anton Pavlovich [Chekhov], "the fishing rods have to be, you know, homemade, crooked. He's made them himself with a pen-knife . . . He has a good cigar . . . Maybe it isn't even that good, but it must be in silver paper . . ."
> Then he stopped speaking, thought a bit and said: "But the main thing is the fishing rods."
> "Then, you know . . . when he, Trigorin, drinks vodka with Masha, I would definitely do it this way, definitely."
> And he stood up, straightened out his vest and awkwardly groaned slightly a couple of times.
> "That's how, you know. I would definitely do it that way. When you've been sitting for a long time, you always want to do that . . ."

K. S. Stanislavsky played Trigorin in the first Art Theatre production of *The Seagull*. He admits in his memoirs that Chekhov was not happy with his interpretation. Stanislavsky's Trigorin dressed like a dandy, while Chekhov had imagined his character in checked pants and shoes with holes in them. " 'And he smokes a cigar this way,' Chekhov continued, and he proceeded to illustrate what he meant."

15. Prov Mikhaylovich Sadovsky (1818-72). What Shchepkin was for Gogol, Sadovsky was for A. N. Ostrovsky, Russia's greatest realist playwright. In the first twenty-eight plays of Ostrovsky staged at the Maly Theatre, Sadovsky took twenty-nine roles. He played Rasplyuyev in the premier performance of *Krechinsky's Wedding* (1855) by A. V. Sukhovo-Kobylin (1817-1903). His interpretation of this rascally incompetent has influenced actors ever since.

Paul Schmidt (in the Harper & Row *Seagull*) writes that Pavel Chadin is probably Shamrayev's invention.

16. Shamrayev combines two Latin proverbs: *De gustibus non disputandum* ("There's no disputing taste") and *De mortuis aut bene aut nihil* ("Speak well of the dead or say nothing at all").

17. Arkadina recites from and Treplyov paraphrases *Hamlet* (act 3, scene 4). The introduction of Shakespeare's play into *The Seagull* would not seem exotic to a Russian audience. Since 1837, when it was staged at the Maly in a new translation by N. A. Polevoy (1796-1846), it had been one of the most popular plays in the repertoire. Treplyov's paraphrase is in fact a verbatim quote from this translation. Hamlet, in his Russian incarnation, became a model for Russians. Thomas G. Winner has written a very useful essay comparing *Hamlet* and *The Seagull*. See "Chekhov's *Sea Gull* and Shakespeare's *Hamlet*" in *The American Slavic and East European Review*, 20 (February 1956).

18. Chekhov does not mean for us to totally dismiss Constantine's play. What would bore an audience in its entirety commands some interest as a fragment. For one thing, it helps set the mood of the play by bringing into prominence the natural setting, and especially the magic lake.

Arkadina says scornfully that Constantine's play imitates the "Decadents," that is, the new European drama, naturalist and symbolist. Chekhov read the European playwrights with interest and sympathy, and he certainly borrowed from them to further his own dramatic purpose. He liked Gerhart Hauptmann's *Lonely Lives*, which explores themes of loneliness and mutual misunderstanding. He was ambivalent about the plays of Ibsen, but it is worthwhile to compare *The Wild Duck* (1886) and *The Seagull*. The plays of Maurice Maeterlinck impressed him deeply because of the purity and depth of feeling in them. Here was real alcohol (see note 27), a drop of which Chekhov adds to Constantine's play to save it from banality.

Chekhov's contemporaries were very aware of the symbolist aspects of *The Seagull*. A. P. Chudakov (*Poetika*

Chekhova [Chekhov's Poetics], Moscow, 1971) quotes the critic A. R. Kugel, who reviewed the play for the *Petersburg Gazette* (*Peterburgskaya gazeta*, no. 289, October 19, 1896): "There are too many realistic details in all this for symbolism, and there's too much symbolist nonsense here for realism" (p. 172). Another critic, writing in 1900, refers to *The Seagull* as "a strange symbolist play with no beginning and no end" (p. 226).

An interesting article by W. G. Jones brings out the way in which symbolism and realism mingle in one detail of *The Seagull*: the lotto game. See "*The Seagull's* Second Symbolist Play-within-a-play" in *The Slavonic and East European Review*, vol. 53, no. 130 (January 1975).

19. A *jeune premier* is the young male lead.

20. In his notes to the Van Itallie translation of *The Seagull* Paul Schmidt writes that Shamrayev's story about Silva and the chorister is in fact a standard joke about bassos. After Shamrayev tells it, the whole company is embarrassed by his attempt to pass it off as original and this accounts for their silence.

21. This is a Russian expression used when an unexpected pause in conversation takes place.

22. Dorn sings "Tell her, pretty flowers" from act 3 of Gounod's *Faust*, the beginning of Siebel's aria, "Faites-lui mes aveux."

23. *Sur l'eau*, written in 1888, records Maupassant's impressions of a visit to the Mediterranean coast that spring. Arkadina reads from a section on the relation of society and the artist. She breaks off before a passage which too clearly suggests her own conquest of Trigorin:

> Like the water which drop by drop wears away the hardest rock, praise falls word by word upon the susceptible heart of the writer. Next, when she feels him touched, stirred, won over by this constant flattery, she isolates him, she severs, little by little, whatever attachments he may have elsewhere, and imperceptibly accustoms him to come to her house, to enjoy himself there, to deposit his thoughts there. The better to acclimatize him in her house, she uses him to best advantage, and prepares his successes, puts him

in the limelight and makes a star of him, and evinces in front of her regular guests the most marked respect for him and an admiration without equal.

And then, feeling that he is an idol, he remains within the temple. He finds it, moreover, most advantageous, for other women will practice their subtlest wiles upon him hoping to snatch him from the one who has captured him.

The passage that Dorn had been reading before the beginning of act 2 resembles Trigorin's description of himself to Nina at the end of it:

The woman who feels herself seized by the bizarre urge to keep a writer around, as one might keep a parrot whose chatter will attract the concierges from next door, must choose between a poet and a novelist. Poets have more of the ideal about them, novelists are less predictable. Poets are more sensitive, novelists more down to earth. It's a matter of taste and temperament. The poet has more personal charm, the novelist is frequently wittier. But the novelist is dangerous in ways that the poet is not: he gnaws, loots, and finds a use for everything that comes his way. You can never be comfortable in his presence, never certain that he won't lay you some day, stark naked, between the pages of a book. His eye is like a pump that sucks up everything, like the hand of a thief that cannot stay idle. Nothing eludes him, he plucks and gathers endlessly; he plucks motions, gestures, motives, everything that passes or happens before him, he gathers every little word, every little action, every little thing. All day long he stocks up on these observations of every kind from which he will make stories to sell, stories to make their rounds everywhere, to be read, chewed over, and talked about by millions. And what is worst of all is that he will make everything true to life, the wretch; despite himself and without realizing it, because he sees clearly and tells what he sees. Try as he might to use his cunning to disguise his characters, people will say, "Did you recognize Monsieur X and Madame Y . . . perfect, aren't they?"

24. Chekhov did understand the concerns of the farmer. See the letter from Melikhovo quoted in note 2.

25. An incident reported in one of Chekhov's letters is traditionally said to have suggested the image of a dead bird to him:

Levitan the painter is staying with me. He and I went out to the woodcock mating area yesterday evening. He fired at a woodcock and the latter, wounded in the wing, fell into a puddle. I picked

106

it up. It had a long beak, large black eyes, and a magnificent
costume. It looked at us in wonder. What could we do with it?
Levitan knit his brow, closed his eyes and begged me with a tremor
in his voice, "Please smash its head against the butt of the rifle."
I said I couldn't. He kept shrugging his shoulders nervously,
twitching his head and begging me. And the woodcock kept looking
on in wonder. I had to obey Levitan and kill it. And while two
idiots went home and sat down to dinner, there was one beautiful,
enamoured creature less in the world. (to Suvorin; April 8, 1892)

26. Poprishchin is the principal character in Gogol's *Notes of a
Madman* (1835).

27. In their memoirs Chekhov's contemporaries often identify
him with Trigorin. This is a mistake, but an understandable
one. Trigorin's speech to Nina does reflect his creator's
observation of himself as a writer. The speech echoes phrases
and sentiments from Chekhov's letters, and in each case the
context is a significant one. The blond and brunette audience,
for instance, crops up in a letter to characterize the youthful
Chekhov's own nervousness over the Petersburg production
of his first serious play. (to Suvorin; January 4, 1889)

The observant and analytical Chekhov obviously took
Maupassant's description of the realistic writer for true coin
(see note 23). He defended the play *Ivanov*, for instance, as
the result of his analysis of real life:

Ivanov and Lvov seemed so alive in my imagination. I'm telling
you the whole truth when I say that they weren't born in my head
out of sea foam or preconceived notions or intellectual pretensions
or by accident. They are the result of observing and studying life.
(to Suvorin; December 30, 1888)

Chekhov also knew in himself both the passion to write and
the disenchantment a writer feels with the finished product:

To tell the truth, even though I did receive the prize [the Pushkin
Prize for literature], I still have not begun my literary career. The
plots for five stories and two novels are languishing away in my
head. One of the novels I conceived so long ago that some of the
characters have grown out of date before my ever getting them down
on paper. I have a whole army of people in my head begging to
be let out and ordered what to do. Everything I've written to date
is nonsense compared with what I would like to have written and
would be overjoyed to be writing. It doesn't make any difference
to me whether I'm writing "The Name-Day Party," or "Lights,"

or a farce, or a letter to a friend — it's all boring, mechanical and vapid and at times I feel chagrined on behalf of some critic who ascribes great significance to, say, my "Lights," I feel as if I'm deceiving him with my writings, just as I deceive many people with my now serious, now inordinately cheerful face. I don't like being a success. The themes sitting around in my head are irritated by and jealous of what I have already written . . . Everything now being written leaves me cold and indifferent, whereas everything stored in my head interests, moves and excites me, from which I conclude that everyone is on the wrong track and I alone know the secret of what needs to be done. That's most likely what all writers think. (to Suvorin; October 27, 1888)

Chekhov gave Trigorin his own love of writing, his passion for analysis, his clear intelligence — and perhaps his feeling of having plundered his own life in search of materials for his art. Trigorin differs from Chekhov in his concept of the writer's duty. Chekhov believed that one should write only about what one knows and understands. From the mid-nineteenth century to the present day every Russian writer has been expected to champion social and political causes in his or her work. Chekhov's range is much greater than Trigorin's — his works are full of instructive and convincing social observation, for instance — but he never wrote simply out of loyalty to a cause. Karlinsky's introduction to *Letters of Anton Chekhov* gives a detailed account of the harassment to which Chekhov was subjected by left and right for his alleged excessive objectivity.

One other line in Trigorin's speech comes from Chekhov's letters: Chekhov applied Trigorin's characterization of his writing as "charming and talented" to himself and the other writers of his generation. He begins this extremely important letter by agreeing with Suvorin's assessment of "Ward Number Six" as "without alcohol." Cheknov means that it is a grimly realistic work, without any hope or positive vision.

Putting "Ward Number Six" and myself aside, let's talk in general terms; that's more interesting. Let's talk about general causes if it doesn't bore you, and let's embrace an entire era. Tell me truthfully now, who among my contemporaries, that is, authors between thirty and forty-five, has given the world a single drop of alcohol? Aren't Korolenko, Nadson and all of today's playwrights lemonade? Have the paintings of Repin and Shishkin turned your head? They're nice, they're talented, [in the Russian these are

Trigorin's exact words translated differently here,] you're delighted by them, but at the same time you can't forget your desire for a smoke. Science and technology are now going through a period of greatness, but for us this is a precarious, sour, dreary period, and we ourselves are sour and dreary . . . The causes do not lie in our stupidity, our insolence or our lack of talent, but in a malady that for an artist is worse than syphilis or sexual impotence. We truly lack a certain something: if you lift up the skirts of our muse, all you see is a flat area. Keep in mind that the writers we call eternal or simply good, the writers who intoxicate us, have one highly important trait in common: they're moving toward something definite and beckon you to follow, and you feel with your entire being, not only with your mind, that they have a certain goal, like the ghost of Hamlet's father, which had a motive for coming and stirring Hamlet's imagination. Depending on their caliber, some have immediate goals — the abolition of serfdom, the liberation of one's country, politics, beauty or simply vodka, as in the case of Denis Davydov [a dashing soldier-poet who fought in the War of 1812] while the goals of others are more remote — God, life after death, the happiness of mankind, etc. The best of them are realistic and describe life as it is, but because each line is saturated with the consciousness of its goal, you feel life as it should be in addition to life as it is, and you are captivated by it. But what about us? Us! We describe life as it is and stop dead right there. We wouldn't lift a hoof if you lit into us with a whip. We have neither immediate nor remote goals, and there is an emptiness in our souls. We have no politics, we don't believe in revolution, there is no God, we're not afraid of ghosts, and I personally am not even afraid of death or blindness. No one who wants nothing, hopes for nothing and fears nothing can be an artist. It may be a malady and it may not; what you call it is not what counts, but we must admit we're in a real fix. I don't know what will become of us in ten or twenty years; maybe things will have changed by then, but for the time being it would be rash to expect anything worthwhile of us, irrespective of whether we're talented or not. We write mechanically, giving in to the long-established order whereby some serve in the military or civil service, others trade and still others write. (to Suvorin; November 25, 1892)

28. From the time of Peter the Great (reigned 1689-1725) Russians in the civil service received ranks and uniforms just as the military did. There were fourteen of these ranks. In his twenty-eight years of service Sorin has made his way up to the fourth, that of *Dejstvitel'nyj Statskij Sovetnik*, Real State Councillor.

29. There were five State or Imperial Theatres: the Mariinsky, Aleksandrinsky and Mikhaylovsky in Petersburg, and the

Bolshoy and Maly in Moscow. From 1842 on, one government agency administered them all, and they suffered from the stuffiness and bureaucratic red tape that afflict state-run institutions. In a period when acting was everything, however, the greatest concentration of good actors remained in the Imperial Theatres, especially in the Maly. It was known as "the House of Shchepkin," in honor of the great actor M. S. Shchepkin (1788-1863). He had created the art of realistic character acting in Russia and inspired a tradition of realism at the Maly which lasted throughout the nineteenth century. Even after the Moscow Art Theatre had successfully performed his *Seagull*, Chekhov submitted his next play, *Uncle Vanya*, to the Maly. Although its director had requested him to do so, a state advisory board of professors in Petersburg rejected the play.

Until 1882 only the Imperial Theatres could publicly produce plays in the capitals. After the abolition of this monopoly a number of commercial theatres sprang up, but no reforms in the drama could originate in them. In 1888, while doing a favor for another playwright, Chekhov saw firsthand the backstage scandals and jealousies that ruled the commercial theatre in the absence of professional standards or love of art. He wrote to his friend Suvorin: "We've got to do what we can to see that the theatre passes from the hands of grocers into the hands of critics and writers." (November 3, 1888)

In the provinces there were only commercial theatres, which multiplied rapidly in the second half of the nineteenth century. Most of their owners cared only about making money. Often completely ignorant themselves, they catered in good conscience to the tastes of the "cultured merchants" who pester Nina. They underpaid their actors or did not pay them at all, and provided the most shabby props for performances. The repertoire of the provincial theatres consisted mostly of melodramas and farces. Plays changed every few days and actors often had no time, even if they felt the inclination, to learn their roles. Despite the gradual improvement that Dorn reports, the general level of acting remained low. Young girls like Nina, who took the theatre seriously, would aspire eventually to act in the capitals. Famous actors like Arkadina did tour the provinces, where they could score enormous successes and dominate the stage. In the mid-seventies in Odessa, a good theatre town, the actress Glebova received fifty-four ovations on her benefit night.

Paul Schmidt makes some interesting remarks about provincial theatre in his notes to the Harper & Row *Seagull*. Two famous Russian novels of the mid-nineteenth century describe the life of a provincial actress. See A. F. Pisemsky's *A Thousand Souls* (1858) and especially M. F. Saltykov-Shchedrin's *The Golovlyov Family* (1872-76), recently issued by Ardis Press in a new translation.

30. M. P. Chekhov reports in his memoirs that his brother Anton attended the theatre in Taganrog frequently after the rest of the family had moved to Moscow. (Chekhov was sixteen at the time.) He especially loved farces and French melodramas, one of which, claims M.P., was entitled *The Mail Robbery*. Historians of the Russian theatre do not seem to know what became of the actors Izmaylov and Suzdaltsev, or indeed who they were.

31. On country estates watchmen on their rounds tapped a stick against a piece of wood both to warn prowlers that the estate was guarded and to assure their employers that they were on the job. The sound emitted was hollow and rhythmical, usually two measured taps followed by a pause and then repeated.

32. Usually this unfinished dramatic poem is called *The Mermaid* in English. In fact, the *rusalka* lives in rivers, and thus ties in more closely with the important water imagery in *The Seagull*. D.S. Mirsky considered *The River Nymph* (1832) "unique, a miracle" and counted it, with two other works by Pushkin, one of the three greatest achievements of Russian poetry. It is a fairy tale of a miller's daughter who, jilted by her princely lover, flings herself into the river. There she becomes a powerful river queen and avenges herself on the prince. The girl's father goes mad after his daughter's death and wanders through the forest. When he meets the prince out hunting, he calls himself a raven. Nina's line, repeated

three times in the last act — "no, that's not right" — is also a quote from *The River Nymph*.

Many poetic passages in *The Seagull* evoke Russian literature. It is as important to the play as *Hamlet, Sur l'eau,* and the works of the so-called Decadents.

33. Lotto is an Italian parlor game, the ancestor of Bingo. Chekhov knew the game well. It was played frequently at Melikhovo.

34. In a letter to A. V. Zhirkevich, a minor writer, Chekhov used these same phrases to illustrate clichés: "Now only lady writers would say 'the placards announced,' 'a face framed with hair.'" (April 2, 1895)

35. Chekhov used images like these in his own story "The Wolf" (1886) and as an illustration of nature description in a letter to his brother Aleksandr that same year:

> In my opinion nature descriptions should be very short and to the point. Commonplaces such as "the setting sun, bathed in the waves of the darkening sea, was flooded with crimson gold" and so on; or "swallows, flying above the surface of the water" — commonplaces like these have to go. In nature description you have to seize on minor details, grouping them so that after you've read them and closed your eyes, you see a picture. For instance, you can get a moonlit night if you write that the glass of a broken bottle glittered on the mill dam like a bright star and the curved black shadow of a dog or wolf rolled by and so forth. (May 10, 1886)

36. These lines come from the epilogue of Turgenev's famous novel *Rudin* (1856).